#Moby-Dick

Or,
The Whale

#Moby-Dick

Or,
The Whale

A Literary Classic Told in Tweets
for the 21st-Century Audience

**Based Upon
Moby-Dick; Or, The Whale
by Herman Melville**

Abridged & reimagined by
Mike Bezemek

Skyhorse Publishing books may be purchased in bulk at special discounts for sales promotion, corporate gifts, fund-raising, or educational purposes. Special editions can also be created to specifi cations. For details, contact the Special Sales Department, Skyhorse Publishing, 307 West 36th Street, 11th Floor, New York, NY 10018 or info@skyhorsepublishing.com.

Skyhorse® and Skyhorse Publishing® are registered trademarks of Skyhorse Publishing, Inc.®, a Delaware corporation.

Visit our website at www.skyhorsepublishing.com.

10 9 8 7 6 5 4 3 2 1

Library of Congress Cataloging-in-Publication Data is available on file

Jacket artwork: iStockphoto

Print ISBN: 978-1-5107-3136-3
Ebook ISBN: 978-1-5107-3137-0

Printed in the United States of America

In token of my appreciation
for her being a kick-ass wife,
this book is inscribed to Ina Seethaler.

CONTENTS

ABOUT *MOBY-DICK*

Published in 1851, *Moby-Dick* is now regularly hailed as one of the greatest works of American literature. However, in its time, the novel was considered a commercial failure and critical flop—sort of like the Ford Edsel, Crystal Pepsi, and that movie based on the board game *Battleship*. Melville had previously written several successful books, mostly romanticized high-seas adventures, including *Typee* (1846) and *Omoo* (1847). But for *Moby-Dick*, Melville had other plans:

> @hermanfromelville (1850)
> Half done with the new book! Getting poetry and truth from blubber is like sap from a frozen maple. (Whales aren't the best dancers.) Yep, gonna be a #strangeone.[1]

Sadly, Melville earned little from the paltry sales of *Moby-Dick*—various reports suggest about $1,300 of total income from around three thousand copies sold in the US and UK.

While Melville continued to write, debt forced him to take employment as a customs inspector in New York. By the time he died in 1891, the book had been out of print for four years.

Meanwhile, contemporary criticism circa 1851–52 ranged widely, with most leaning toward the negative. Critics couldn't even agree what to call the *thing*, with some complaining it was like three books discordantly crammed together. A high-seas whaling drama? An encyclopedic reference for whale info resembling a bunch of collected magazine how-to articles? A digressive philosophy tome on the meaning of life with ample insertions of phallic humor—whale penis tunic, anyone?

@fancynewyorkmagazine (1852)
Melville? Shoulda wrote one or two books tops. (Forget this guy.) And Moby-Dick? Gonna be in the dictionary under "American Lit, Sucky examples of . . ."[2]

@charlestonsouthernreview (1852)
Readers may dig the whaling scenes in Moby-Dick, but otherwise it's sad stuff. Ahab is a monstrous BORE! Melville should be committed.[3]

@londonliterarygazette (1851)
If Moby-Dick is a novel, then for Thanksgiving Melville must serve a skeletal chicken over-stuffed with cetalogical facts.[4]

Still, some early reviewers did mention positive qualities that would come to be considered among *Moby-Dick*'s most cherished attributes. Chief among these, the countless themes, meanings, and symbols that allow for so many diverse interpretations—even if various elements offended some readers' sensibilities.

About *Moby-Dick*

@johnbullinlondon (1851)
Philosophy in whales? Poetry in blubber? Extraordinary!
But prepare, dear reader, for uncouth & heathenish
stabs at sacred religions #unnecessary[5]

@willyoungnyalbion (1851)
Look, Melville is clearly a genius and Moby-Dick is worth
reading—FYI, just skim the dialogue & skip a page now
and then.[6]

@londonukspectator (1851)
Moby-Dick is an identity crisis with good characters.
Ahab is melodramatic, though. And Ishmael DIES? Wtf!
So how does he tell the story then? #hello[7]

For modern readers, Ishmael as the lone survivor is common knowledge. But even that was up for debate in the 1850s. Reason being, the original British version, published by Richard Bentley, was quite different from the complete American version that's known to modern readers, published by Harper & Brothers. First, the British title was changed to *The Whale*. Second, several hundred passages were removed by Bentley's editors, most likely for being considered offensive. And, third, the epilogue—which informs the reader of Ishmael's solo escape—was entirely omitted.

After Melville's death, a critical reappraisal of his work began around the turn of the twentieth century and continues to this day. The basic gist? *Moby-Dick* was ahead of its time—sort of like Athenian democracy, Jules Verne's *Nautilus* submarine, and the world's first internet search butler Ask Jeeves. Not only critics but literature scholars and famous authors rallied, with varying levels of enthusiasm, to Melville's masterpiece.

#Moby-Dick; Or, The Whale

@therealdhlawrence (1923)
The last great hunt! Nobody clowns more than Melville, even in a wonderful and strange book like Moby-Dick. Of course the whale is a symbol.[8]

@carlclintvandoren (1924)
Melville's style is a galloping thoroughbred! Allegoric Ahab has 100 meanings! Moby-Dick is greatness for endless debate! i.e. #fewreaders[9]

@williamcfaulkner (1927)
What Greek-like simplicity: a white whale signals doom, a despot drags the ship down with him; there's death for a man. I wish I wrote it (but I'm not a sailor).[10]

@ernesthemingway99 (1949)
I can count on one hand the writers I've still gotta beat. Melville gets the pointer finger.[11]

@johnniesteinbeck (1963)
To the loud critics and the loudest ones, a great novel with a name like Moby-DICK was enough to make them guffaw with ochre rage #haters #criticsofwrath[12]

Today, near universal curiosity toward *Moby-Dick* endures, with new analyses and interpretations offered regularly. Scholars and readers continue to debate: *WTF is this thing?* A high-drama whaling tale? An encyclopedic parable? A homo-erotic thriller? An examination of racist deceptions? A complex human tragicomedy?

And what does it *mean*? That hatred is predestined in the hearts of men? That unchecked masculinity leads to a toxic desire toward domination? That some lurking resentment is eternally directed toward religious orthodoxy, societal order, cultural customs, and the concept of home, or the port, which offers "safety, comfort, hearthstone, supper, warm blankets, friends, all that's kind to our mortalities?" And in turn, these resentments encourage those willing and able to partake in violence or evil while fleeing from "all havens astern?" Certainly, it's not one single thing. To each reader, *Moby-Dick* is something different, based upon their unique perceptions and interpretation of Melville's 206,000-word epic.

Regarding Melville, might the author be the most tragic character in the drama that is *Moby-Dick*? After all, in his lifetime, *Moby-Dick* and Melville himself were largely ignored, unrecognized as the master he has since become—kind of like Jane Austen, Vincent Van Gogh, or that director who made *Plan 9 From Outer Space*.

Perhaps. Perhaps not. There was one Melville contemporary who recognized the novel's immense value; who praised and defended it publicly—and privately to Melville; who had kind things to say, not just about the novel, but about Melville in general; who was one of the most famous and successful American authors of the period:

@nathanielhawthorne (1856)
My man Mel's all toil and adventure! He is too honest! Too courageous! If he were religious? He'd be way too religious! Dude's worth immortality.[13]

DISCLAIMER

The contents of this book—tweets, hashtags, taglines, handles, etc.—are a product of the author's imagination and are in no way affiliated with Twitter or any of its users. This book is not authorized or sponsored by Twitter, Inc., or any other person or entity owning or controlling rights in the Twitter name, trademark, or copyrights.

#Moby-Dick

or,
The Whale

ETYMOLOGY

@ijustlovelexicons:

From the Danish word HVAL, or "arch," plus the German word WALLEN, or "to roll," equals #WHALE! (Ok, are we done here? Can we move on now?)[14]

EXTRACTS

@yesthatmosesfromgoshen:

And GOD created big 'ol whales. #boss[15]

♥ ▣ ↻ ☰

@williamshakes1564:

Straight uppeth like a whale.[16]

♥ ▣ ↻ ☰

2

@*hobbesofmalmesbury:*

Sketch a nation as a whale, states are just people on maps. #fake[17]

♥   💬   ↻   ≡

@*antoniodeulloa:*

Whale breath is SO stank. It can make you cray.[18]

♥   💬   ↻   ≡

@*therealcaptaincook:*

Thought we saw a rock but it was a dead whale. (lol!) Some Asiatics (luv the Asiatics btw) killed it and were hiding like we couldn't see 'em. #wesawthem[19]

♥   💬   ↻   ≡

@*barongeorgescuvier:*

Whales got boobs, but no feet.[20]

♥   💬   ↻   ≡

@*reverendhenrycheever:*

A whale just fell right on top of this guy! So I asked, is he dead? And they're all, "yeah, he dead . . ."[21]

♥　　　💬　　　↻　　　≡

@*whaleboatcruiser:*

Everyone knows that whaling crews rarely return on the same ship they departed with. #theshipsalllookthesame[22]

♥　　　💬　　　↻　　　≡

THE TWEETS

Ishmael here! I went broke in NYC. 😢 Super bored with land (damp drizzly soul). I'm going to sea! #callme #whalingvoyage[23]

In New Bedford for a few days, waiting for a ferry to Nantucket. The inn is run by Peter "COFFIN?" I hope that's not an omen.[24]

Ugh—all beds are taken. I'm supposed to share with a tattooed cannibal?! At first he pulled a tomahawk but now we're cool. This Queequeg fella? #solidguy[25]

WTF! I woke up with Queg spooning me. Odd dude. He dresses in reverse: hat → boots → pants → shirt. Shaves with a harpoon. #whatabadass #oraMURDERER[26]

There's a LOT of sailors at breakfast. Everyone is tan and awkwardly silent. FYI, Queg's harpoon is also his utensil (he eats only beefsteaks). #classic[27]

Walkin' past the docks to church. There's savages strolling, gents in tails, lumberjacks, country bumpkins. ALL seek glory with a lance. Plus hot chicks errrywhere.[28]

The chapel is full of moody fishermen and sad widows. There are plaques for the deceased: one overboard, Patagonia; one dragged into the Pacific; one killed near Japan. #YOLO[29]

The pulpit suspends like a ship's prow. The priest climbs up by rope ladder! Hmm . . . Wrinkled face, young soul, old habits? I'm thinking ex-sailor. #nailedit[30]

Pretty cool sermon: "Sinful Jonah fled to sea, but was thrown overboard into god's storm. Jonah got ate by a huge whale, but he gratefully repented and was puked onto land!" #happyending[31]

So, my new buddy Queg's a real George Wash with face tats. We smoked up and worshipped Yojo, his wooden idol—lol! #wenotmarried[32]

Couldn't sleep, so we lit a lamp and smoked in bed. Wonder, does the landlord have fire insurance? Queg told me his story . . . [33]

♥   💬   ↻   ≡

. . . a Pacific island prince, Queg was curious about Christianity. So he sunk his canoe and boarded a whaler. (Learned even Christians can be miserable and wicked.) He joins my voyage![34]

♥   💬   ↻   ≡

Finally, we're on a schooner for Nantucket! Queg gets nasty looks from taunting bumpkins. But when one rude dude fell overboard? Queg still dove in and saved him. 💪[35]

♥   💬   ↻   ≡

About Nantucket: It's a sandy anthill for sea hermits who war with salty mastodons and spend years on the terraqueous globe like landless gulls. #WEIRDOS[36]

♥   💬   ↻   ≡

Another inn, another omen? Outside, two black pots hang from a mast. Inside, it's all "clam or cod?" Chowder for dinner, breakfast, lunch. Smoked herring for dessert. 🔪 [37]

♥　　💬　　↻　　≡

Queg's idol Yojo decreed I select our ship, so I searched the docks all day until . . . the Pequod! Named for an extinct Massachusetts tribe & supposedly a whale ate the captain's leg. #perfect[38]

♥　　💬　　↻　　≡

Returning to the inn, our door is locked! I knock, whisper, shout. The keeper fears suicide, so I bust down the door. Inside, Queg's in a trance with Yojo on his head. #thisguy[39]

♥　　💬　　↻　　≡

I brought Queg to the Pequod, so owners could size him up. He harpooned a tar spot about the size of an eye! Got hired on the spot. Big guy signed with two circles, like this: ∞ [40]

♥　　💬　　↻　　≡

Back on shore, a bum shouted at us: "God pity the souls who ship with Old Thunder! Ye don't know about Ahab's lost leg!" Well, thanks for the late warning, man.[41]

Tomorrow we sail! The Pequod is loaded with beef, bread, & sails. #thebasics. And we got spares for everything—except a captain. Has anyone seen this Ahab dude?[42]

Good morning! Queg and I boarded at dawn. Thought I saw five sailors in the mist, but the ship was quiet. Maybe it was just shadows? #whatevs[43]

And we're off! Man the capstan! Raise anchor! Set sails! Brrr . . . ocean spray encases us in ice. Someone mentioned a hot Nantucket supper in three years. Wait! Did he say three?[44]

Our ship fights a gale blowin' hard toward shore. Sure, the sea is scary. But it offers a god-like freedom. I'd rather die in the howl than in a bed on shore. #amirite?[45]

Us whalers pioneer uncharted seas & lands, while lamps on shore burn sperm oil to our glory! A ship is our Harvard! 🎓 The USA is #1 in whaling, baby![46]

Fun fact: What anoints the hair of British kings at coronation? Yep, that would be sperm oil. (And btw, hair gel is not cool for REAL American guys.)[47]

I met the fellas today. The chief mate is Starbuck, and he's here to kill whales for a living, not be killed by them for theirs. #dropthemike[48]

The third mate is Flask, he's a fearless little guy with a chip on his shoulder. And second mate Stubb is a calm pipe smoker—the jaws of death are like his easy chair. #waychill[49]

♥   💬   ↻   ☰

There's three harpooners on board. You know Queg. Next is Daggoo, a 6'5" African who makes Flask look like a chess piece . . . [50]

♥   💬   ↻   ☰

. . . and finally Tashtego, a proud Indian warrior with long hair, who swapped his bow and arrows for cold iron. What a bunch of characters! #wegonnahavefun[51]

♥   💬   ↻   ☰

We're sailing south to flee winter, it's day 4, and guess who? Ahab! He's standing like bronze atop an ivory leg. Got scars 'cross his face, grey wavy hair, a squinty grin.[52]

♥   💬   ↻   ☰

On warm nights, our captain paces. The guy sleeps like three hours, tops. His bone leg hammering the deck wakes us all up. Great—Ahab has insomnia. #fml[53]

Every night, Ahab does two things. He visits the hold (wonder why) and smokes on deck. But tonight he's moody—tossed his pipe into the sea. #dramaqueen.[54]

Stubb awoke & told of a weird-ass dream: Ahab kicked Stubb, who kicked Ahab, who turned into a pyramid (wha-what?). A humpbacked merman explained it's all good to be kicked by great men. #checksout[55]

Is the whale a fish? Linnaeus says NO (warm blood, lungs, eyelids, horizontal tail). But me? I'm old-fashioned. Experts can #suckit. The Bible says YES.[56]

FYI—I luv talking about whales! So your sperm whale (aka anvil head) is globe's largest creature. Super awesome, dangerous, valuable, but what a goofy-ass name. . . . [57]

The right whale (aka Greenland) was the first whale hunted by man. But its oil is inferior to spermaceti. A real "baleine-ordinaire." #rimshot #yeahispeakfrench[58]

The humpback (aka elephant) whale is playful and laidback. Often on the North American coast. Gotta HUGE hump, so pretty creative name. 😜 . . . [59]

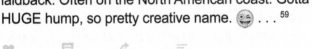

The narwhal (aka unicorn) whale has a horn up to ten feet long! Used to be known as an antidote for fainting, #forreals. Now it's just known for a really big tusk . . . [60]

The killer whale is a savage. It bites other whales to death. But what a stoopid name. We are all killers, on land and sea. #sharks #bonapartes . . . [61]

Ok, ok. I'll quit listing whales! But my list is unfinished, like a cathedral. Man, I hope I never complete anything. Tweets are just drafts of drafts. #slacker4lyfe[62]

Hey, did you know that 100 years ago, the chief harpooner split command with the captain? Not for us. We just have Ahab. And he is soooo shaggy. #takeabathbro[63]

A typical lunch onboard? Ahab cuts meat for the mates, who peck nervously, like their jawbones might snap. #relax! Afterward, the harpooners come in and eat like barbarians. #slowdownguys[64]

Ok, so kinda crazy, but the Pequod has no crow's nest—just two sticks?! It's like standing on bull's horns while daydreaming. And, YES, I'm a shitty guard. #redhanded[65]

Ahab gathered the crew today: "Ya heard of the white whale? That SOB ate my leg. Gold for Moby Dick!" Everyone was all cheering, passing grog, drinking from harpoon sockets. #partay[66]

So . . . I overheard Ahab at the window: "I can't enjoy setting suns. I know iron, not gold. My skull is steel. I'll dismember my dismemberer. I'm kinda cray like that."[67]

Next, Starbuck was talking to himself at the mast: "Great. Tied to a madman captain and heathen crew. Round the watery world for vengeance upon a whale. Yay me."[68]

During the first watch, Stubb wondered what his honey at home is doing without him. Crying? Partying with harpooners? Dude choked while laughing. #relationshipgoals[69]

By midnight we were singing! A French sailor danced. Iceland just stood there. Manxman said the black sky is an omen. Daggoo said why fear black? Spain called race card, pulled a knife. #bonding[70]

Ever since Ahab's speech, us crewmen have traded wild rumors. The white whale swims in two oceans at once! It can't be killed! It can ram boats! Ahab's feud is ours! #monomania[71]

Hey, is anyone else terrified by the color white? Think about it: polar bears? Great white sharks? Albinos? Hello, the dead? Ghosts? Snow? Tropical nuns . . . ?[72]

Hark! I heard a noise in the night. A flapping sail? Maybe stomach gasses? A Quaker knitting on shore? Or just a cough? Sounds to me like a sleeper turning. Someone is in the hold. #stowaway[73]

How do we find a single whale among four oceans? Ahab's chart has tides, winds, currents, foods, and migrations. The man sleeps with clenched fists and wakes with bloody palms.[74]

You should know: only one in fifty deaths by whale are reported. Whales will drag and destroy vessels. The Essex was sunk in 1820. #dontwaitup[75]

I think Ahab only wants Moby Dick, but he knows us men want money. So he told us to keep a bright eye for all and report even porpoises. (#porpoisessuck)[76]

Queg and I wove a mat today! I shuttled threads through fixed yarns. Queg's errant sword formed a motley fabric. This is our #FATE.[77]

"Thar she blows!" Spouts rise! Flukes flash! The school dives and the Pequod chases—but what? 😃 Ahab is surrounded by five shadows, seemingly formed from air.[78]

The three harpoon boats lowered—plus a fourth?! The captain's spare, now rowed by five Parsis, including leader Fedallah, wearing turban and jacket. The shadow crew.[79]

From Starbuck's boat, Queg tossed his harpoon! The beast rose and swamped us, #uhoh. A squall formed and we drifted through dense fog until morning. #whereweat[80]

Suddenly, the Pequod burst from fog! As it bore down, we dove aside and our boat was dragged under. Everyone thought we perished? Not. This. Time.[81]

♥ 💬 ↻ ≡

Back aboard the Pequod, I had to ask: Is this a typical event? All said YES. (Man, the universe is like a big April fool's joke.) So, I went below to write my will.[82]

♥ 💬 ↻ ≡

Some backstory: wise whalers have long argued should a captain risk his life in the chase? Pequod's owners said NO, so Ahab smuggled the Parsis aboard to row him. #sneakysneaky[83]

♥ 💬 ↻ ≡

Many nights on watch, a silvery jet bursts from the sea in the moonlight. 🐋 We've chased from the Atlantic into the Indian Ocean, but never caught this spirit spout. Could it be Moby Dick? Luring us to remote & savage seas? #socold[84]

♥ 💬 ↻ ≡

We just passed the Albatross, out of Nantucket and homebound after four years at sea. Ahab hollered, "Address our mail to the Pacific Ocean!" #roundtheworld[85]

♥   🗩   ↻   ≡

So, usually, passing whalers have a visit (aka "gam"). The homeward captain provides intel on the hunting grounds. The outbound captain delivers mail and some less-out-of-date newspapers. #buddysystem[86]

♥   🗩   ↻   ≡

Just met with the Town Ho. Their crazy story? A fight between a hand and mate! A near mutiny! The hand planned murder! But the mate was swallowed by Moby Dick. 📖 #andscene[87]

♥   🗩   ↻   ≡

Ok, back me up. Most whale paintings are way off. Is it a vine stalk? Anaconda? Squash! Log raft! Aquatic camel! But why? #whalesdontpose4portraits[88]

♥   🗩   ↻   ≡

And so few paint the hunt! The little-experienced French have the best—worthy of Versailles. But us Americans? Too busy hunting. #toobusylivin[89]

♥   💬   ↻   ≡

Us Americans do other things, like carving whale teeth, wooden whales on forecastles, brass door knockers, weather vanes. We 🖤 us some #whaleAmericana.[90]

♥   💬   ↻   ≡

Can I tell ya'll about brit? That be meadows of yellow krill. Plus, the sea? A symbol of man's horror. And land is like peace & joy. Guys, the great flood is still ongoing. Two-thirds of the world? #OCEAN[91]

♥   💬   ↻   ≡

Today we spotted a white mass lazily rising! Moby Dick? We chased, but found only a giant squid. That shit is sperm whale prey, not ours. 🖐[92]

♥   💬   ↻   ≡

FYI—each boat has a whale line that's 1,200 feet of rope, coiled in tubs. When fast (harpooned) to a whale, it whizzes like a steam engine. #hangmansnoose[93]

Finally, we spotted a whale & chased! Tashtego's harpoon got fast and (warning! NSFW! Rated R! Get your barf bags!) Stubb speared the creature till its heart exploded. Ours is a #bloodybiz.[94]

Um, so harpooning is tough stuff. It takes a strong arm to strike the first iron from like 30 feet. Only one in ten throws are successful. #dontquityourdayjob[95]

Oh and there's a second iron that's connected to the first harpoon and thrown right afterward. This one often fails and becomes a dangling terror that flops around until the whale is dead. #nobiggie[96]

Tonight, sharks are biting at the whale carcass tied beside the Pequod. Onboard, Stubb is pecking at a whale steak. #sogross. He complains it's overdone. Now the cook wishes the whale ate Stubb and not the other way around.[97]

Quick question: is it weird for Stubb to feed on the creature that feeds our lamps? Is a 100-foot meat pie not appetizing? Whale meat is rich stuff and aren't we all carnivores?  #discuss[98]

The night watch are stabbing at sharks gathered round the carcass. The men aim for skulls but often miss, bloodying the water. The sharks snap at their wounds, creating an #entrailouroboros. #deepstuffhuh[99]

So, when we cut into the whale, the Pequod runs red like we're sacrificing 10,000 oxen. The blubber hook skins the thing, and every sailor becomes a butcher.  How about some #overtime?[100]

About that blubber: it's like a magical blanket that keeps whales comfortable in all seas. Cool at the equator, warm at the poles. #whalesaresocool #tohunt[101]

Once our task is complete, the carcass floats astern for the vultures. Like a white phantom, distant ships think it's a rocky shoal. Amend your charts! #fairwarning[102]

Oh, btw, we kept the head. And whale decapitation ain't easy. The head is a third the whale's weight. Like a sphynx. Oh, great! Now Ahab is talking to it. WTF?[103]

We met the Jeroboam today. They had a crazy Shaker deckhand who refused to work, declared himself a prophet, and now he overrules the captain. #whynot[104]

Forgot to mention, yesterday my man Queg straddled the carcass, inserted the blubber hook, and jogged on it like a treadmill as it spun. Me? I held a safety rope from the ship. #teamwork[105]

We killed a right whale today! Fedallah said a second head must balance the first. (Makes our ship unsinkable? #myth) The crew whispers Fedallah is the devil; he tucks away his tail.[106]

So, a sperm whale head is shaped like a Roman chariot. Has its eyes fore and aft. A lower jaw like a joist with 42 teeth. #hottie[107]

A right whale's head is like a leather loafer with barnacles for a crown and baleen plates like venetian blinds to strain brit. Eats with its mouth open. #nottie[108]

The sperm whale's forehead is a dead wall, a battering ram, twenty feet of boneless wad and oil. Even our sharpest harpoons rebound. #dudesamonster[109]

Inside the head is the Heidelberg Tun, a case for prized oil. 500 pounds in the biggest sperm whales. The stuff crystalizes in air, so we try to not spill. #weprofessionals[110]

OMG! Tashtego was just bucketing oil and slipped headfirst into the Tun! Hooks ripped from the ship and the head sank. Guess who dove in and saved him? Queg. #boss[111]

Did you know a sperm whale's got NO nose, NO face, just a brow wide as a prairie. Like Shakespeare but without any features (or all those plays). A genius doing nuthin' to prove it. 😎[112]

At the back of its skull? A ten-foot brain. But isn't backbone the true sign of character? The sperm whale's spinal cord has serious girth. #sizematters[113]

Met the Jungfrau today, whose captain visited for oil (no whales taken #thatsux). But suddenly, one spouted! Both ships chased, and we won! But the carcass sank. #all4nothing[114]

Trivia time! What do Perseus, St. George, Hercules, Jonah, and Vishnu all have in common? Anyone? This is not a trick question. #yougotthis[115]

. . . Whales! 🐋[116]

Us whalemen question Jonah's story. He was held in a whale's belly, not mouth? Eaten in the Mediterranean Sea and puked at Ninevah? Round the Cape of Good Hope in three days? #fishtale[117]

Check this out! We call it pitchpoling. Yesterday, a boat was being dragged by a whale, so Stubb hurled a spear on a rope repeatedly into the beast until it spouted blood. Then sat back and watched the monster die. #smooth[118]

Here are three rumors about blowholes: Only one breath per hour! The jet can blind! The "steam" rising from its forehead is a sign of smart thoughts! And for me, as well (after six cups hot tea in my attic in August).[119]

The tail has five motions: a forward flap; a sweep and slap on the surface; a strike against boats; and lifting its flukes to dive. No fishy wiggles. We're talking manly horizontal propulsion.[120]

We passed beyond the Straits of Sunda today. While we chased a herd, Malay pirates chased us! We wet our sails and dropped 'em astern. #peaceout[121]

We lowered boats as the whales panicked and scattered. Queg got fast and our boat was dragged into the herd, gashing the sea white as we dodged beasts.[122]

While being towed, we hurled druggs (harpoons roped to barrels) at errant whales to wing them, so we might return later and kill all we can. But for all our efforts, we got only one. #welldarn[123]

Our harpoon pulled free, and we floated in a quiet lake of cows and calves. Like dogs, they snuffled our gunwales. We petted their foreheads, scratched their backs. #socute[124]

Soon, others gathered 'round the doubloon. Starbuck saw the Trinity. Stubb saw the whole life of a man. Flask saw cigar money. And Pip saw the Pequod . . . resting on the sea floor.[137]

We visited the Sam Enderby of London today. Their captain lost his arm to Moby Dick! Now he wants no more. Ahab shouted "Where?" Their doc tried to take Ahab's pulse, who shoved back. They pointed us east.[138]

Regarding Enderby & Sons, they were the first English whalers, first in general to hunt the Pacific. They carried so much beef, pork, bread, butter, cheese, beer, and gin—had little time to fish.[139]

So I know A LOT about the inner sperm whale. I dissected a cub on deck once and measured a skeleton on Tranque Island. Tattooed the stats on my arm. #not2brag #inked[140]

With sperm whale schools it's either 1) young bulls who joust with lower jaws, or 2) lady whales traveling with just one full-grown male escort. #luckyguy[125]

Rules of the sea: a whale fastened by a cable or cobweb is claimed. A loose fish (whale struck but lost) is fair game. And single ladies? America in 1492? Human rights? The whole wide world? #loosefish[126]

Laws in England dictate a whale is crown property. #yep. The tail goes to the queen—I guess for her mermaid costume? The head goes to the King— cuz he's equally dense? #commonsense[127]

We met the Rosebud, a French ship towing a fetid carcass. Stubb told 'em it's blasted. He offered to dispose, but instead we stole the corpse. Free #ambergris![128]

Regarding ambergris, it's a fragrant wax used in the perfumery. No joke: a byproduct of dyspepsia from the bowels of a sick whale. It is worn by #fineladies. #glamglam[129]

Our cabin boy Pip replaced an injured rower today. First whale we struck? Pip fell overboard and got tangled in the line. So, we cut and lost the whale! Second whale? Same thing! So we let Pip float for hours. #comeonkid[130]

On deck, we squeezed lumps of oil from a whale we caught, often catching each other's hands. #brotherlylove. Meanwhile, down in the blubber room, barefoot men spaded whale flesh while the ship rolled. #toesRscarce[131]

We use everything from the whale! For example, the mincer makes a cassock from the whales "jet black cone" (if you know what I mean). He cuts leg and neck holes and slips inside. #runway #usewhatyougot #yesthepenis[132]

Our tryworks are a brick kiln for boiling the minc blubber on high seas. While steering last night, I drifted off and jerked the wheel. Hot oil flew everywhere! #mybad[133]

Not to talk smack, but merchantmen have to dress, eat, and stumble through the dark. Not us whalemen. We burn oil lamps through the roughest nights. #doitwiththelightson[134]

After many months at sea, we are dialed: 1) warm oil into casks 2) roll 'em like a landslide the hold 3) scrub, brush, and clean the ship every 96 hours, a young life's old routine aga

The gold doubloon offered for Moby Dick is nailed to the mast. Today Ahab visited it. Ab three Andes peaks engraved on the coin? saw three Ahabs. #humble[136]

Drum roll, please . . . the stats: the skeleton was 72-feet long, meaning 90 alive! Ten ribs, each 6–8 feet long! The skull is 20-feet long, the backbone is 50 feet! Forty vertebrae tapered to marbles. #childsplay[141]

Pre-Adamite whale fossils have spanned the globe. In Alabama, 1842, they found a full skeleton. Slaves thought it a fallen angel. Docs thought it a reptile. Regardless, whales pre-date the Pharaohs.[142]

Some critics warn of extinction? Ha! One whaling ship takes only 40, not forty thousand like buffalo hunters. Whales are like elephants. We still got plenty in 1850. #comeon[143]

Returning from the Enderby, Ahab broke his peg leg in the boat. Turns out, that's the second time. Before our voyage, it snapped and smacked his groin. #OUCH. So, Moby Dick ate Ahab's leg AND kicked him in the balls. [144]

Our carpenter does it all! Paints oars, pulls teeth, builds whalebone birdcages and new pegs. He's like our pocket knife—we take him by the legs and lower him like tweezers. #shoutout[145]

♥   📰   ↻   ☰

Ahab asked the Carpenter: "Can you build me a new man? Fifty feet in socks, chest like a tunnel, legs with roots, skylights for eyes. By the way, I still feel my lost leg . . ." #crickets #awkward[146]

♥   📰   ↻   ☰

A leaky cask sent Starbuck to Ahab, asking for a port. Ahab pulled a musket. "Heave to? Hell nah. Let it leak." Starbuck talked back, "Let Ahab beware of Ahab." Our captain gave in, and we emptied the hold.[147]

♥   📰   ↻   ☰

During a hot search, Queg got a bad fever. He asked the carpenter for a canoe-shaped coffin. Then Queg climbed in—with his harpoon, Yojo, & pillow—and pulled the lid. #mypal #RIP . . .[148]

♥   📰   ↻   ☰

. . . but wait! Queg recalled a small duty he had ashore. He rallied! Emerged! Yawned and stretched! Says he's healed and ready for a fight! Turned the coffin into his sea chest. #makessense[149]

We've reached the Pacific! Hello, great southern sea! 1,000 leagues of blue! Sweet mystery! Earth's tide-beating heart! Of course Ahab ruined it: "Stern, all. The white whale spouts blood."[150]

Meet Perth, our limping blacksmith. The man had wife, kids, home—but lost all (to a burglar called the bottle) plus his toes on a winter stumble. 🫤 So Perth went a whaling! #upside[151]

Ahab asked Perth: "Can you smooth my brow, buddy? Nope? Fine, then make me a harpoon with racehorse studs, tempered in blood, and use my razors for barbs." #projecttime![152]

We reached the Japanese whaling grounds today and floated on smooth swells. The ocean looked like a velvet paw that hides fangs. But Stubb was in a super jolly mood. #iwantwhathehad[153]

We crossed paths with the Bachelor, homebound and bulging with oil. Even had casks in their crow's nest! Their captain invited us over, but Ahab never lets us do fun things. #dadmove[154]

We just killed FOUR whales! And Ahab got one. He watched it roll belly up, called it a water-locked worshipper praying to the sun. #umokay #dramatic[155]

Through the night, Ahab's boat floated with the corpse. I overheard Fedallah tell Ahab, "No coffin for you. To die it will take two hearses, one made of wood. Only hemp can kill ye." #peptalk[156]

Back aboard the Pequod at high noon, Ahab got mad while calculating latitude. He said the sun and quadrant can't find a white whale, so he trampled the device! #woah. "Square in!" he shouted. Equator season has arrived. [157]

A typhoon hit tonight! Waves! Lightning! The masts glowed! A boat cracked! The harpoons blazed! The corpusants! Ahab grabbed a fiery dart and blew it out like a candle. #baller[158]

During first watch, Starbuck wanted to strike the main topsail. But Ahab said: "Strike nothing! Lash everything! Take medicine!" #unsolicitedadvice[159]

At the forecastle, Stubb said lashing anchors is like tying our hands behind our back. Flask said the Pequod needs a bigger insurance policy.[160]

Aloft, Tashtego lashed a yard, complaining: "Ok, thunder, we get it. This is way too much. Who wants thunder? We want rum." #manknowswhathewants[161]

While Ahab slept, Starbuck grabbed a musket and pondered murder. Sail through the night by dead reckoning, without lightning rods, risking thirty lives? But Starbuck couldn't do it. He returned to the deck.  [162]

This morning, the ship was pointing east—but the sun was astern? The storm turned our compasses —a bad omen. The crew shuddered as Ahab hammered new needles. We turned into the wind.[163]

To gauge our speed, Ahab called to heave the log and line. Manxman said it's old and will snap, but Ahab insisted. Overboard went the log. And the line? It snapped. #warnedya[164]

What could possibly go wrong next? Well, how about Pip going crazy? He thinks he's still swimming at sea. Ahab took pity and invited Pip to bunk in his cabin. #uhhh #wut[165]

And today we lost a watchman. He fell in. #shit. We tossed the buoy, but both sank. Now we don't even have a life buoy. So, Queg offered his coffin to the carpenter. #couldwork[166]

On deck, Ahab watched the carpenter hammering. "One day, legs. Now a buoy. You heathenish scamp, is a coffin like an immortality preserver? . . . So, hey, are you done yet?" #smalltalk[167]

We met the Rachel. The captain's son was lost when a boat was dragged off by Moby Dick. He begs for our help. But Ahab, like an anvil, refuses. #whataguy #stonecold[168]

Meanwhile, Pip's identity crisis continues . . .
Pip wanted to help on deck, but Ahab refused
(said it's cuz Pip be crazy, not cuz Pip is black).
#theyalike[169]

Ahab no longer trusts the look-outs, so he was
hoisted up the main mast. Aloft only ten minutes,
a sea hawk snatched his hat and flew off.
#itsthelittlethings[170]

Today we passed the Delight, with a funeral in
progress. Moby Dick crushed a boat! A body is
retired to sea and the splash slapped the Pequod.
A ghostly baptism. #creepy[171]

Ahab: "Forty years at sea, only three on peaceful
land. A wedding pillow with one dent, a widow with
husband alive, a son with only tales. A cruel power
commands me."[172]

Aloft, Ahab spotted a hump like snow! Birds circled and landed on a lance rising from the white whale's back. We dropped three boats, as the whale arced and dove! #herewego[173]

From a boat, I peered into the sea: a white spot? → two rows of teeth? → a marble tomb? → a jaw biting! → our boat splitting! → Ahab fell overboard! → Moby Dick circled! → the Pequod descended and ran him off. #wechase[174]

The Pequod flew onward, like a cannon ball, through the night and into morning. The crew was frenzied, we clung to the rigging. Like one man, not thirty. We were ripe for fate. #gangsta[175]

The whale breached with a mountain of foam! It glittered and glared like a glacier! Visible from 7 miles! A white salmon tossed to heaven! #letsgokillit[176]

Moby Dick rushed toward our boats, which darted irons. Lines tangled and two boats crashed together. Moby Dick flipped Ahab's with a headbutt and swam off—but Fedallah was snagged by a rope and dragged under. #gone[177]

Moby Dick rushed toward our boats, which darted irons. Lines tangled and two boats crashed together. Moby Dick flipped Ahab's with a headbutt and swam off—but Fedallah was snagged by a rope and dragged under. #gone[177]

For three full days, we've chased this whale. Aboard the Pequod, at noon, the sea was empty. Looking behind, we over-sailed Moby Dick! "Now he chases me," said Ahab. "Not I him."[178]

The Pequod turned back as we readied the spare boats. Starbuck's eyes teared up. He shook Ahab's hand and begged him not to go 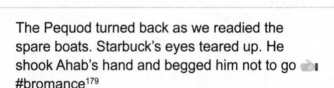 #bromance[179]

As we rowed ahead, sharks circled! A hum rumbled! Moby Dick rose—with Fedallah's torn body lashed to its back. A Leviathan hearse. #remindmewhyimhereagain[180]

Moby Dick swatted the other boats, but left Ahab's untouched, and swam off. Starbuck shouted from the Pequod: "See! It seeketh thou not! Quit stalking, man!" #word[181]

Our oars shrank from shark bites as we rowed Ahab forward. Other men swam for the ship to make new irons. Tashtego climbed our flagless mainmast to nail a new one. #priorities[183]

And hark! Ahab heard. He called it all off. We rowed back to the Pequod and got rum drunk. We sailed homeward to that hot Nantucket supper we were promised. #theend #jk #yeahright[182]

Ahab darted his iron! It sank to its socket into the whale's flank. Moby Dick slapped the boat and flew! The whale line snapped! An oarsman fell astern![184]

Moby Dick rammed the Pequod. Men and timbers reeled! Water poured through the breach! Ahab called out: "The ship! Made of wood! The second hearse!"[185]

"From hell's ♥, I stab at thee!" Ahab hurled the final harpoon. As Moby Dick darted away, the whale line snagged around Ahab's neck and he shot down into the depths. #hemp[186]

Like a gaseous fata morgana, the Pequod, its masts, and the final boat, all sunk into the whirlpool, like #phantoms.[187]

As it went down, Tashtego kept hammering the flag, even as a taunting seahawk landed and was nailed to the mast. All sunk beneath, and the sea rolled white like it did 5,000 years ago.[188]

The Tweets

I alone escaped to tell this tale. I was the oarsman who was thrown from Ahab's boat, #luckyme. BTW, can anyone pick me up? (I'm the guy floating on a wooden coffin in the middle of the Pacific Ocean.) [189]

Nevermind, it's cool. Here comes the Rachel. Still searching for her lost children, but gonna find only me. #anotherorphan[190]

APPENDIX

Endnotes

1   Melville's letter to Richard Henry Dana, Jr, 1850. "About the 'whaling voyage'—I am half way in the work, & am very glad your suggestion so jumps with mine. It will be a strange sort of a book, tho', I fear; blubber is blubber you know; tho' you may get oil out of it, the poetry runs as hard as sap from a frozen maple tree;—& to cook the thing up, one must needs throw in a little fancy, which from the nature of the thing, must be an ungainly as the gambols of the whales themselves. Yet I mean to give the truth of the thing, spite of this."

2   *New York United States Magazine and Democratic Review*, January 1852. "The truth is, Mr. Melville has survived his reputation. If he had been contented with writing one or two books, he might have been famous, but his vanity has

destroyed all his chances for immortality, or even of a good name with his own generation . . . We have no intention of quoting any passages just now from Moby Dick . . . But if there are any of our readers who wish to find examples of bad rhetoric, involved syntax, stilted sentiment and incoherent English, we will take the liberty of recommending to them this precious volume of Mr. Melville's."

3   *Charleston Southern Quarterly Review*, January 1852. "In all the scenes where the whale is the performer or the sufferer, the delineation and action are highly vivid and exciting. In all other aspects, the book is sad stuff, dull and dreary, or ridiculous . . . his Mad Captain . . . is a monstrous bore . . . the ravings of Mr. Melville himself, meant for eloquent declamation, are such as would justify a writ *de lunatico* against all the parties." ·

4   *London Literary Gazette*, December 1851. "The author has read up laboriously to make a show of cetalogical learning . . . He uses it as stuffing to fill out his skeleton story. Bad stuffing it makes, serving only to try the patience of his readers, and to tempt them to wish both him and his whales at the bottom of an unfathomable sea . . . The story of this novel scarcely deserves the name."

5   *London John Bull*, October 1851. "Of all the extraordinary books from the pen of Herman Melville this is out and out the most extraordinary. Who would have looked for philosophy in whales, or for poetry in blubber . . . To give anything like an outline of the narrative woven together from materials seemingly so uncouth . . . must be prepared, however, to hear much on board that singularly-tenanted ship which grates upon civilized ears; some heathenish, and worse than heathenish talk is calculated to give even more serious offence . . . and it is all the greater pity, that he should have defaced his pages by occasional thrusts against revealed religion which add nothing to the interest

Appendix

of his story, and cannot but shock readers accustomed to a reverent treatment of whatever is associated with sacred subjects."

6   William Young, in *New York Albion*, November 1851. "Herman Melville is a practical and practised sea-novelist, and that what comes from his pen will be worth the reading. And so indeed is *Moby-Dick*, and not lacking much of being a great work . . . the production of a man of genius . . . It is only when Mr. Melville puts words into the mouths of these living and moving beings, that his cunning fails him, and the illusion passes away . . . There is neverthelesss in it, as we have already hinted, abundant choice reading for those who can skip a page now and then, judiciously . . ."

7   *London Spectator*, October 1851. "This sea novel is a singular medley of naval observation, magazine article writing, satiric reflection upon the conventionalisms of civilized life, and rhapsody run mad . . . The "marvellous" injures the book by disjointing the narrative, as well as by its inherent want of interest, at least as managed by Mr. Melville . . . The strongest point of the book is its "characters." Ahab, indeed, is a melodramatic exaggeration, and Ishmael is little more than a mouth-piece; but the harpooners, the mates, and several of the seamen, are truthful portraitures of the sailor as modified by the whaling service . . . It is a canon with some critics that nothing should be introduced into a novel which it is physically impossible for the writer to have known: thus, he must not describe the conversation of miners in a pit if they *all* perish. Mr. Melville hardly steers clear of this rule, and he continually violates another, by beginning in the autobiographical form and changing ad libitum into the narrative . . . ."

8   D. H. Lawrence, "Herman Melville's Moby Dick," from *Studies in Classic American Literature*. "A hunt. The last great hunt. For what? For Moby Dick, the huge white

sperm whale: who is old, hoary, monstrous, and swims alone; who is unspeakably terrible in his wrath, having so often been attacked; and snow-white. Of course he is a symbol . . . Nobody can be more clownish, more clumsy and sententiously in bad taste, than Herman Melville, even in a great book like *Moby Dick* . . . So ends one of the strangest and most wonderful books in the world, closing up its mystery and its tortured symbolism."

9   Carl Van Doren, "Mr. Melville's 'Moby Dick.'" "Its variety is one measure of its greatness, as is also that profound vitality which will make it long capable of being wrangled over by rival critics who can no more come to agreement than they can about the meaning of experience itself . . . Ahab has a hundred symbolical or allegorical implications. He writes with the energy of a man who is tirelessly alert, even in his most learned chapters nipping the heels of his exposition so that it caracoles like a thoroughbred . . . Though he may have limited his audience for "Moby Dick" by his mannerisms, he almost certainly has written a book which, despite them and partly by reason of them, will awaken half frantic enthusiasms in numerous bosoms for many years to come."

10   William Faulkner, interview with *Chicago Tribune*, July 1927. "I think that the book which I put down with the unqualified thought 'I wish I had written that' is Moby Dick. The Greek-like simplicity of it: a man of forceful character driven by his somber nature and his bleak heritage, bent on his own destruction and dragging his immediate world down with him with a despotic and utter disregard of them as individuals . . . And the symbol of their doom: a White Whale. There's a death for a man, now . . ."

11   Citation lost. 😜

12   Ibid.

Appendix

13 Nathaniel Hawthore, *English Notebooks*, 1856. "A week ago last Monday, Herman Melville came to see me at the Consulate . . . He is thus far on his way to Constantinople. I do not wonder that he found it necessary to take an airing through the world, after so many years of toilsome pen-labor, following upon so wild and adventurous a youth as his was . . . Melville, as he always does, began to reason of Providence and futurity, and of everything else that lies beyond human ken . . . He can neither believe, nor be comfortable in his unbelief . . . he is too honest and courageous not to try to do one or the other. If he were a religious man, he would be one of the most truly religious and reverential; he has a very high and noble nature, and is better worth immortality than the most of us."

14 Etymology. "The pale usher . . . He was every dusting his old lexicons and grammars . . . it somehow mildly reminded him of his mortality . . . 'WHALE. *** *Sw. and Dan.* hval . . . *arched or vaulted* . . . *Dut. And Ger.* Wallen . . . *to roll, to wallow.*'"

15 Extracts. "'*And God created great whales.*' Genesis."

16 Extracts. "'*Very like a whale.*' Hamlet."

17 Extracts. "'By art is created that great Leviathan, called a Commonwealth or State—(in Latin, Civitas) which is but an artificial man.' Opening sentence of Hobbes's Leviathan."

18 Extracts. "****'and the breath of the whale is frequently attended with such an insupportable smell, as to bring on a disorder of the brain.' Ulloa's South America."

19 Extracts. "'In the afternoon we saw what was supposed to be a rock, but it was found to be a dead whale, which some Asiatics had killed, and were then towing ashore. They seemed to endeavor to conceal themselves behind

the whale, in order to avoid being seen by us.' Cook's Voyages."

20 Extracts. "'The whale is a mammiferous animal without hind feet.' Baron Cuvier."

21 Extracts. "'The whale fell directly over him, and probably killed him in a moment.' 'The Whale and His Captors, or The Whaleman's Adventures and the Whale's Biography, Gathered on the Homeward Cruise of the Commodore Preble.' By Rev. Henry T. Cheever."

22 Extracts. "'It is generally well known that out of the crews of Whaling vessels (American) few ever return in the ships on board of which they departed.' Cruise in a Whale Boat."

23 Chapter I: Loomings. "Call me Ishmael . . . having little or no money in my purse, and nothing particular to interest me on shore, I thought I would sail around and see the watery part of the world . . . whenever it is a damp drizzly November in my soul . . . I account it high time to get to sea . . . after having repeatedly smelt the sea as a merchant sailor, I should now take it into my head to go on a whaling voyage . . ."

24 Chapter II: The Carpet Bag. "Quitting the good city of old Manhatto, I duly arrived in New Bedford . . . my mind was made up to sail in no other than a Nantucket craft . . . having a night, a day, and still another night . . . ere I could embark for my destined port . . . I at last came to a dim sort of light not far from the docks . . . looking up, saw a swinging sign . . . 'The Spouter Inn: —Peter Coffin.' Coffin?— Spouter?—Rather ominous in that particular connexion . . ."

25 Chapter III: The Spouter-Inn. "I sought the landlord . . . his house was full, not a bed unoccupied . . . 'But avast,' he added . . . 'you haint no objections to sharing with a harpooneer's blanket, have ye?' . . . At last I slid off

into a light doze . . . when I heard a heavy footfall in the passage . . . Such a face! . . . with large, blackish looking squares . . . heavens! Look at that tomahawk! . . . 'Who-e debel you?'—he at last said—'you no speak-e, dam-me, I kill-e.' . . . the landlord came into the room light in hand . . . 'Queequeg here wouldn't harm a hair of your head.' . . . 'You gettee in,' he added, motioning to me with his Tomahawk . . . in not only a civil but a really kind and charitable way . . . For all his tattooings he was on the whole a clean, comely cannibal . . . I turned in, and never slept better in my life."

26 Chapter IV: The Counterpane. "Upon waking next morning about daylight, I found Queequeg's arm thrown over me in the most loving and affectionate manner. You had almost thought I had been his wife . . . He commenced dressing at top by donning his beaver hat . . . and then—still minus his trowsers—he hunted up his boots . . . I begged him . . . to get into his pantaloons as soon as possible. He complied . . . He then donned his waistcoast . . . lo and behold, he takes the harpoon . . . begins a vigorous scraping, or rather harpooning of his cheeks."

27 Chapter V: Breakfast. "The bar-room was now full of the boarders . . . They were nearly all whalemen . . . You could plainly tell how long each one had been ashore. This young fellow's healthy cheek is like a sun-toasted pear in hue . . . That man next him looks a few shades lighter . . . In the complexion of a third still lingers a tropical tawn . . . nearly every man maintained a profound silence . . . they looked embarrassed . . . But as for Queequeg . . . bringing his harpoon into breakfast with him . . . reaching over the table with it . . . and grappling the beefsteaks towards him . . . he eschewed coffee and hot rolls . . ."

28 Chapter VI: The Street. ". . . taking my first daylight stroll . . . actual cannibals stand chatting at street corner: savages

outright . . . all athirst for gain and glory in the fishery . . . fellows who have felled forests, and now seek to drop the axe and snatch the whale-lance . . . Look there! That chap strutting round the corner. He wears a beaver hat and swallow-tailed coat . . . a country-bred one—I mean a downright bumpkin dandy . . . And the women of New Bedford, they bloom like their own red roses."

29   Chapter VII: The Chapel. ". . . a Whalemen's Chapel, and few are the moody fishermen . . . who fail to make a Sunday visit . . . and Sailor's wives and widows . . . several marble tablets . . . masoned into the wall . . . lost overboard near the Isle of Desolation, off Patagonia . . . towed out of sight by a whale, on the off-shore ground in the Pacific . . . killed by a sperm whale on the coast of Japan . . . somehow I grew merry again . . . Delightful inducements to embark . . . Yes, there is death in this business of whaling . . . But what then? Methinks we have hugely mistaken this matter of Life and Death."

30   Chapter VIII: The Pulpit. ". . . the famous Father Mapple . . . had been a sailor and harpooner in his youth . . . among all the fissures of his wrinkles, there shone certain mild gleams of a newly developing bloom—the spring verdure peeping forth even beneath February's snow . . . there were certain engrafted clerical peculiarities about him, imputable to that adventurous maritime life he had led . . . the pulpit without a stairs, substituting a perpendicular side ladder, like those used in mounting a ship . . . of red worsted man-ropes . . . hand over hand, mounted the steps as if ascending the main-top of his vessel . . . deliberately drag up the ladder step by step . . . Its paneled front was in likeness of a ship's bluff bows . . ."

31   Chapter IX: The Sermon. ". . . the sin of this son of Amittai was in his willful disobedience of the command of God . . . to flee from Him . . . seeks a ship that's bound for Tarshish

. . . A dreadful storm comes on, the ship is like to break . . . Jonah taken up as an anchor and dropped into the sea . . . goes down in the whirling heart of such a masterless commotion . . . into the yawning jaws awaiting him, and the whale shoots-to all his ivory teeth . . . Jonah prayed unto the Lord . . . feels that his dreadful punishment is just . . . here, shipmates, is true and faithful repentance . . . how pleasing to God was this conduct in Jonah . . . God spake unto the fish . . . the whale came breeching up . . . and 'vomited out Jonah onto dry land.'"

32 Chapter X: A Bosom Friend. "Savage though he was, and hideously marred about the face . . . his head was phrenologically an excellent one . . . it reminded me of General Washington's head, as seen in popular busts of him . . . Queequeg was George Washington cannibalistically developed . . . I began to feel myself mysteriously drawn to him . . . I'll try a Pagan friend, thought I, since Christian kindness has proved but hollow courtesy . . . I proposed a social smoke; and, producing his pouch and tomahawk, he quietly offered me a puff . . . he pressed his forehead against mine, clasped me round the waist, and said that henceforth we were married; meaning, in his country's phrase, that we were bosom friends . . . He then went about his evening prayers, took out his idol . . . How then could I unite with this wild idolator in worshipping his piece of wood? But what is worship? . . . I must turn idolator . . . So I kindled the shavings; helped prop up the innocent little idol; offered him burnt biscuit with Queequeg; salamed before him twice or thrice; kissed his nose; and that done, we undressed and went to bed."

33 Chapter XI: Nightgown. "Nor did I at all object to the hint from Quequeeg that perhaps it were best to strike a light, seeing that we were so wide awake; and besides, he felt a strong desire to have a few quiet puffs from his Toma-

hawk . . . though I had felt such a strong repugnance to his smoking in bed the night before . . . I no more felt unduly concerned for the landlord's policy of insurance . . . he now spoke of his native island . . ."

34   Chapter XII: Biographical. ". . . a native of Kokovoko, an island far away to the West and South . . . in Queequeg's ambitious soul lurked a strong desire to see something more of Christendom than a specimen whaler or two. His father was a High Chief, a King . . . A Sag Harbor ship visited his father's bay . . . he padded off to a distant strait . . . gained her side . . . capsized and sank his canoe . . . he was actuated by a profound desire to learn among the Christians, the arts whereby to make his people still happier than they were . . . But, alas! The practices of whalemen soon convinced him that even Christians could be both miserable and wicked; infinitely more than all his father's heathens . . . seeing what the sailors did . . . how they spent their wages . . . gave it up for lost . . . I asked him what might be his immediate purpose . . . He answers, to go to sea again . . . I told him that whaling was my own design . . . He at once resolved to accompany me . . . I joyously assented . . ."

35   Chapter XIII: Wheelbarrow. ". . . we stood on board the schooner. Hoisting sail, it glided down the Acushnet river . . . jeering glances of the passengers . . . Queequeg caught one of these young saplings mimicking him behind his back . . . the brawny savage . . . sent him high up bodily into the air . . . the fellow landed with bursting lungs upon his feet . . . The poor fellow who Queequeg had handled so roughly, was swept overboard . . . Queequeg, stripped to his waist, darted from the side with a long living arc of a leap . . . he rose again, one arm still striking out, and with the other dragging a lifeless form . . . poor bumpkin was soon restored."

36 Chapter XIV: Nantucket: ". . . a mere hillock, and elbow of sand . . . in all seasons and all oceans declared everlasting war with the mightiest animated mass that survived the flood . . . salt-sea Mastodon . . . Nantucketers, those sea hermits, issuing from their ant hill . . . two thirds of this terraqueous globe are for the Nantucketers . . . For years he knows not land . . . it smells like another world, more strangely than the moon would to an Earthsman. With the landless gull, that at sunset folds her wings and is rocked to sleep between billows . . ."

37 Chapter XV: Chowder. "The landlord of the Spouter Inn had recommended us to his cousin Hosea Hussey of the Try Pots . . . Two enormous wooden pots painted black, and suspended by asses' ears, swung from the cross-trees of an old top mast . . . looked not a little like a gallows . . . It's ominous, thinks I . . . Mrs. Hussey . . . ushered us into a little room . . . "Clam or Cod?" . . . when that smoking chowder came in, the mystery was delightfully explained . . . Chowder for breakfast, and chowder for dinner, and chowder for supper, till you began to look for fish-bones coming through your clothes . . . 'let's have a couple of smoked herring by way of variety' . . ."

38 Chapter XVI: The Ship: "Queequeg now gave me to understand . . . Yojo earnestly enjoined that the selection of the ship should rest wholly with me . . . I was obliged to acquiesce . . . I learnt that there were three ships up for three-years' voyages . . . Pequod . . . was the name of a celebrated tribe of Massachusets Indians, now extinct . . . going on board . . . this was the very ship for us . . . 'Clap eye on Captain Ahab, young man, and thou wilt find that he has only one leg . . . Lost by a whale! . . . devoured, chewed up, crunched by the monstrousest parmacety that ever chipped a boat.'"

39 Chapter XVII: The Ramadan. "Towards evening . . . I went up to his room and knocked . . . but no answer. I tried to open it, but it was fastened inside . . . 'Queequeg,' I said softly . . . 'Queequeg! Queequeg!'—all still . . . Mrs. Hussey soon appeared . . . told me that Queequeg's harpoon was missing. 'He's killed himself,' she cried . . . 'Have to burst it open,' said I . . . and with a sudden bodily rush dashed myself full against the mark . . . there sat Queequeg, altogether cool and self-collected; right in the middle of the room; squatting on his hams and holding Yojo on top of his head . . . But as soon as the first glimpse of sun entered the window, up he got . . . his Ramadan was over."

40 Chapter XVIII: His Mark. "'I say, Quohog, or whatever your name is, did you ever stand in the head of a whaleboat? Did you ever strike a fish?' Without saying a word, Queequeg . . . jumped on the bulwarks . . . and poising his harpoon, cried out . . . 'spose him one whale eye, den' . . . he darted the iron . . . and struck the glistening tar spot . . . 'Quick, I say, you Bildad, and get the ship's papers. We must have Hedgehog there, I mean Quohog, in one of our boats' . . . Queequeg . . . taking the offered pen, copied upon the paper, in the proper place, an exact counterpart of a queer round figure which was tattooed upon his arm . . ."

41 Chapter XIX: The Prophet. "Queequeg and I had just left the Pequod . . . a stranger . . . leveled his massive forefinger at the vessel in question . . . 'ye haven't seen Old Thunder yet, have ye? . . . ye've heard tell about the leg, and how he lost it . . . All about it, eh—sure you do?—all?' . . . the beggar-like stranger . . . said: 'ye've shipped, have ye? Names down on the papers? Well, well, what's signed, is signed . . . some sailors or other must go with him, I suppose . . . God pity, 'em!' . . . his ambiguous, half-hinting, half-revealing, shrouded sort of talk, now begat in me all

kinds of vague wonderments and half-apprehensions, and all connected with the Pequod . . . and the voyage we had bound ourselves to sail."

42 Chapter XX: All Astir. ". . . new sails were coming on board . . . Just so with whaling, which necessitates a three-years' housekeeping . . . Hence, the spare boats . . . spare everything, almost, but a spare Captain . . . the heaviest storage of the Pequod had been almost completed; comprising her beef, bread, water . . . often I asked about Ahab . . . some time the next day the ship would certainly sail."

43 Chapter XXI: Going Aboard. "It was nearly six o'clock, but only grey imperfect misty day, when we drew nigh the wharf. 'There are some sailors running ahead there, if I see right,' said I to Queequeg, 'it can't be shadows' . . . 'I thought I did see four or five men; but it was too dim to be sure.' . . . stepping on board the Pequod, we found everything in profound quiet, not a soul moving . . . 'Those sailors we saw, Queequeg, where can they have gone to?'"

44 Chapter XXII: Merry Christmas. "'Man the capstan! Blood and thunder!—jump!'—was the next command, and the crew sprang for the handspikes . . . At last the anchor was up, the sails were set, and off we glided . . . we found ourselves almost broad upon the wintry ocean, whose freezing spray cased us in ice . . . 'and this day three years I'll have a hot supper smoking for ye in old Nantucket. Hurrah and away!' . . . we gave three heavy-hearted cheers, and blindly plunged like fate into the lone Atlantic."

45 Chapter XXIII: The Lee Shore. ". . . in the port is safety, comfort, hearthstone, supper, warm blankets, friends, all that's kind to our mortalities. But in the gale, the port, the land, is that ship's direst jeopardy; she must fly all hospitality . . . fights 'gainst the very winds that fain would blow her homeward . . . the wildest winds of heaven and earth

conspire to cast her on the treacherous, slavish shore . . . better is it to perish in that howling infinite . . . straight up, leaps thy apotheosis!"

46 Chapter XXIV: The Advocate. ". . . for almost all the tapers, lamps, and candles that burn round the glove, burn, as before so many shrines, to our glory! . . . how comes it that we whalemen of America now outnumber all the rest of the banded whalemen in the world . . . For many years past the whale-ship has been the pioneer in ferreting out the remotest and least known parts of the earth. She has explored seas and archipelagoes which had no chart . . . I prospectively ascribe all the honor and the glory to whaling; for a whaleship was my Yale College and my Harvard."

47 Chapter XXV: Postscript. "I would fain advance naught but substantiated facts . . . in common life we esteem but meanly and contemptibly a fellow who anoints his hair . . . a mature man who uses hair-oil, unless medicinally, that man has probably got a quoggy spot in him . . . what kind of oil is used at coronations? . . . sperm oil in its unmanufactured, unpolluted state . . . Think of that, ye loyal Britons! We whalemen supply your kings and queens with coronation stuff!"

48 Chapter XXVI: Knights and Squires. "The chief mate of the Pequod was Starbuck . . . For, thought Starbuck, I am here in this critical ocean to kill whales for my living, and not to be killed by them for theirs . . . the courage of this Starbuck which could, nevertheless, still flourish, must indeed have been extreme."

49 Chapter XXVII: Knights and Squires. "Stubb was the second mate . . . and while engaged in the most imminent crisis of the chase, toiling away, calm and collected as a journeyman joiner engaged for the year . . . Long usage had, for this Stubb, converted the jaws of death into an

easy chair . . . For, like his nose, his short, black little pipe was one of the regular features of his face . . . The third mate was Flask . . . A short, stout, ruddy young fellow, very pugnacious concerning whales, who somehow seemed to think that the great Leviathans had personally and hereditarily affronted him . . . This ignorant, unconscious fearlessness of his made him a little waggish in the matter of whales . . ."

50 Chapter XXVII: Knights and Squires. ". . . we set down who the Pequod's harpooners were . . . Queequeg is already known . . . Third among the harpooners was Daggoo, a gigantic, coal-black negro-savage . . . never having been anywhere in the world but in Africa, Nantucket, and the pagan harbors . . . erect as a giraffe, moved about the decks in all the pomp of six feet five in his socks . . . Ahasuerus Daggoo, was the Squire of little Flask who looked like a chess-man beside him."

51 Chapter XXVII: Knights and Squires. "Next was Tashtego, an unmixed Indian from Gay Head . . . Tashtego's long, lean, sable hair, his high cheek bones, and black rounding eyes . . . proclaimed him an inheritor of the unvitiated blood of those proud warrior hunters . . . Tashtego now hunted in the wake of the great whales of the sea; the unerring harpoon of the son fitly replacing the infallible arrow of the sires . . . they were nearly all Islanders in the Pequod, *Isolatoes* too, I call such . . . what a set these Isolatoes were!"

52 Chapter XXVIII: Ahab. "For several days after leaving Nantucket, nothing above hatches was seen of Captain Ahab . . . for a space we had biting Polar weather, though all the time running away from it to the southward; and by every degree and minute of latitude which we sailed, gradually leaving that merciless winter . . . Captain Ahab stood upon his quarter-deck . . . His whole high, broad form, seemed made of solid bronze . . . Threading its way out from

among his grey hairs, and continuing right down one side of his tawny scorched face and neck, till it disappeared in his clothing, you saw a slender rod-like mark, lividly whitish . . . this overbearing grimness was owing to the barbaric white leg upon which he partly stood . . . this ivory leg had at sea been fashioned from the polished bone of the Sperm Whale's jaw . . . More than once did he put forth the faint blossom of a look, in any other man, would have soon flowered out in a smile."

53   Chapter XXIX: Enter Ahab; To Him, Stubb. ". . . the still mild hours of eve came on . . . Old age is always wakeful . . . [Ahab] usually abstained from patrolling the quarter-deck, because to his wearied mates, seeking repose within six inches of his ivory heel, such would have been the rever-berating crack and din of that bony step, that their dreams would have been of the crunching teeth of sharks. But once, the mood was on him too deep for common regard-ings; and as with heavy, lumber-like pace he was mea-suring the ship from taffrail to mainmast, Stubb, the odd second mate, came up from below . . . 'He ain't in his bed now, either, more than three hours out of the twenty-four, and he don't sleep then.'"

54   Chapter XXIX: Enter Ahab; To Him, Stubb. "'[Ahab's] full of riddles; I wonder what he goes into the after hold for, every night . . . '" Chapter XXX: The Pipe. "Lighting the pipe at binnacle lamp and planting the stool on the weather side of the deck, he sat and smoked . . . 'What business have I with this pipe? This thing meant for sereness, to send up mild white vapors among mild white hairs, not among torn iron-grey locks like mine. I'll smoke no more—' He tossed the still lighted pipe into the sea."

55   Chapter XXXI: Queen Mab. "'Such a queer dream . . . You know the old man's ivory leg, well I dreamed he kicked me with it . . . presto! Ahab seemed a pyramid . . . a sort of

badger-haired old merman, with a hump on his back, takes me by the shoulders . . . 'you were kicked by a great man, and with a beautiful ivory leg, Stubb. It's an honor' . . ."

56 Chapter XXXII: Cetology. "The uncertain, unsettled condition of this science of Cetology is in the very vestibule attested by the fact, that in some quarters it still remains a moot point whether a whale be a fish . . . Linnaeus declares, 'I hereby separate the whales from the fish . . . On account of their warm bilocular heart, their lungs, their moveable eyelids' . . . I submitted all this to my friends . . . both messmates of mine in a certain voyage, and they united in the opinion that the reasons set forth were altogether insufficient. Charley profanely hinted they were humbug. Be it known that, waiving all argument, I take the good old fashioned ground that the whale is a fish, and call upon holy Jonah to back me . . . To be short, then, a whale is a *spouting fish with a horizontal tail*."

57 Chapter XXXII: Cetology. "Now, then, come the grand divisions of the entire whale host . . . *(Sperm Whale)* . . . vaguely known as . . . the Anvil-Headed Whale . . . is, without doubt, the largest inhabitant of the globe; the most formidable of all whales to encounter; the most majestic in aspect; and lastly, by far the most valuable in commerce . . . All his peculiarities will, in many other places, be enlarged upon. It is chiefly with his name that I now have to do. Philogically considered, it is absurd."

58 Chapter XXXII: Cetology. "*(Right Whale)* . . . the most venerable of the Leviathans, being the one first regulary hunted by man. It yields . . . oil specially known as 'whale oil,' an inferior article in commerce. Among the fishermen, he is indiscriminately designated . . . the Greenland Whale . . . the Baliene Ordinaire of the French whalemen."

59 Chapter XXXII: Cetology. *"(Hump Back)* . . . is often seen on the northern American coast . . . you might call him the Elephant . . . At any rate, the popular name for him does not sufficiently distinguish him, since the Sperm Whale also has a hump, though a smaller one . . . the most gamesome and lighthearted of all the whales . . ."

60 Chapter XXXII: Cetology. *"(Narwhale)*..its horn averages five feet, though some exceed ten, and even attain to fifteen. Strictly speaking, this horn is but a lengthened tusk . . . I have heard it called . . . the Unicorn Whale . . . was in the ancient days regarded as the great antidote against poison . . . It was also distilled to a volatile salts for fainting ladies . . ."

61 Chapter XXXII: Cetology. *"(Killer)* . . . He is very savage—a sort of Feegee fish. He sometimes takes the great Folio Whales by the lip, and hangs there like a leech, till the mighty brute is worried to death . . . Exception might be taken to the name . . . For we are all killers, on land and on sea; Bonapartes and Sharks included."

62 Chapter XXXII: Cetology. "Finally: It was stated at the outset, that this system would not be here, and at once, perfected. You cannot but plainly see that I have kept my word. But I now leave my Cetological System standing thus unfinished, even as the great Cathedral of Cologne was left, with the crane still standing upon the top of the uncompleted tower . . . God keep me from ever completing anything. This whole book is but a draught—nay, but the draught of a draught."

63 Chapter XXXIII: The Specksynder. ". . . in the old Dutch Fishery, two centuries and more ago, the command of a whale-ship was not wholly lodged in the person now called the captain, but was divided between him and an office called the Specksynder . . . equivalent to Chief

Harpooner . . . this old Dutch official is still retained, but his former dignity is sadly abridged . . . in the American Fisherey he is not only an important officer in the boat . . . But Ahab, my Captain, still moves before me in all his Nantucket grimness and shagginess . . ."

64 Chapter XXXIV: The Cabin-Table. "It is noon . . . the steward . . . announces dinner . . . each officer waited to be served . . . their intent eyes fastened upon the old man's knife, as he carved the chief dish . . . After their departure . . . the three harpooners were bidden to the feast . . . While their masters, the mates, seemed afraid of the sound of the hinges of their own jaws, the harpooners chewed their food with such a relish . . . though these barbarians dined in the cabin . . ."

65 Chapter XXXV: The Mast-Head. ". . . in due rotation with the other seamen my first mast-head came round . . . In the serene weather of the tropics it is exceedingly pleasant the mast-head; nay, to a dreamy meditative man it is delight-ful . . . Your most usual point of perch is the head of the t'gallant-mast, where you stand upon two thin parallel stilts (almost peculiar to whale-men) called the t'gallant cross-trees. Here, tossed about by the sea, the beginner feels about as cosy as he would standing on bull's horns . . . it is much to be deplored that the mast-heads of a southern whale ship are unprovided with those enviable little tents or pulpits, called *crow's-nests* . . . Let me make a clean breast of it here, and frankly admit that I kept sorry guard."

66 Chapter XXXVI: The Quarter Deck. "When the entire ship's company were assembled . . . Ahab . . . addressed them thus:—'All ye mast-headers have before now heard me give orders about a white whale. Look ye! d'ye see this Spanish ounce of gold? . . . Whosoever of ye raises me a white-headed whale with a wrinkled brow and a crooked jaw; whosoever of ye raises me that white-headed whale;

with three holes punctured in his starboard fluke—look ye, whosoever of ye raises me that same white whale, he shall have this gold ounce, my boys!' 'Huzza! Huzza!' cried the seamen . . . 'aye, my hearties all round; it was Moby Dick that dismasted me; Moby Dick that brought me to this dead stump I stand on now' . . . I'll chase him round Good Hope, and round the Horn, and round the Norway Maelstrom, and round perdition's flames before I give him up . . . Steward! go draw the great measure of grog . . . Drink and pass!' he cried, handing the heavy charged flagon to the nearest seamen . . . Forthwith, slowly going from one officer to the other, he brimmed the harpoon sockets with the fiery waters from the pewter . . . The long, barbed steel goblets were lifted; and to cries and maledictions against the white whale, the spirits were simultaneously quaffed down with a hiss."

67   Chapter XXXVI: Sunset. "[*The cabin; by the stern windows; Ahab sitting alone, and gazing out*] . . . 'The diver sun—slow dived from noon,—goes down . . . 'Tis iron—that I know—not gold . . . my brain seems to beat against the solid metal; aye, steel skull, mine . . . Oh! time was, when as the sunrise nobly spurred me, so the sunset soothed. No more . . . I'm demoniac, I am madness maddened! . . . I now prophesy that I will dismember my dismemberer . . . come and see if ye can swerve me. Swerve me?"

68   Chapter XXXVI: Sunset. ". . . 'I came here to hunt whales, not my commander's vengeance." Chapter XXXVII: Dusk. "[*By the Mainmast; Starbuck leaning against it*] 'My soul is more than matched; she's overmanned and by a madman! . . . I think I see his impious end; but feel that I must help him to it. Will I, nill I, the ineffable thing has tied me to him; tows me with a cable I have no knife to cut . . . Oh! I plainly see my miserable office,—to obey, rebelling . . . The hated whale has the round watery world to swim

in . . . Oh, god! to sail with such a heathen crew that have small touch of human mothers in them! The white whale is their demigorgon."

69 Chapter XXXIX: First Night-Watch. "'Ha! ha! ha! ha! hem! clear my throat! . . . What's my juicy little pear at home doing now? Crying its eyes out?—Giving a party to the last arrived harpooners, I dare say, gay as a frigate's pennant, and so am I—fa, la! lirra, skirra!'"

70 Chapter XL: Midnight, Forecastle. "Harpooners and Sailors . . . all singing in chorus . . . French Sailor: 'Hist, boys! let's have a jig or two' . . . Iceland Sailor: 'I don't like your floor, maty; it's too springy to my taste. I'm used to ice-floors. I'm sorry to throw cold water on the subject; but excuse me.' . . . Old Manx Sailor: 'Our captain has his birth-mark; look yonder, boys, there's another in the sky—lurid-like, ye see, all else pitch black.' . . . Dagoo: 'What of that? Who's afraid of black's afraid of me! I'm quarried out of it!' Spanish Sailor: (*Aside.*) 'He wants to bully, ah!—the old grudge makes me touchy. (Advancing.) Aye, harpooner, thy race is the undeniable dark side of mankind—devilish dark at that. No offence.' All: 'A row! a row! a row!' English Sailor: 'Fair play! Snatch the Spaniard's knife!'"

71 Chapter XLI: Moby Dick. "I, Ishmael, was one of that crew; my shouts had gone up with the rest; my oath had been welded with theirs . . . Ahab's quenchless feud seemed mine . . . the outblown rumors of the White Whale did in the end incorporate . . . half-formed foetal suggestion of supernatural agencies . . . the unearthly conceit that Moby Dick was ubiquitous; that he had actually been encountered in opposite latitudes at once and the same instant of time . . . some whalemen should go still further in their superstitions; declaring Moby Dick not only ubiquitous, but immortal . . . though groves of spears should be planted in his flanks, he would still swim away unharmed

. . . he had several times been known to turn round suddenly, and, bearing down upon them, either stave their boats to splinters, or drive them back in consternation to their ship . . . the mad secret of his unabated rage bolted up and keyed in him, Ahab had purposely sailed upon the present voyage with the one only and all-engrossing object of hunting the White Whale . . . Such a crew, so officered, seemed specially picked and packed by some infernal fatality to help him to his monomaniac revenge . . . For one, I gave myself up to the abandonment of the time and the place; but while yet all a-rush to encounter the whale . . ."

72 Chapter XLII: The Whiteness of the Whale. "It was the whiteness of the whale that above all things appalled me . . . when divorced from more kindly associations, and coupled with any object terrible in itself, to heighten that terror to the furthest bounds. Witness the white bear of the poles, and the white shark of the tropics . . . the Albino man so peculiar repels and often shocks the eye . . . the one visible quality in the aspect of the dead which most appalls the gazer, is the marble pallor lingering there . . . Not even in our superstitions do we fail to throw the same snowy mantle round our phantoms; all ghosts rising in a milk-white fog . . . why does the passing mention of a White Friar or a White Nun, evoke such an eyeless statue in the soul . . . an unbounded prairie sheeted with driven snow, no shadow of tree or twig to break the fixed trance of whiteness . . ."

73 Chapter XLIII: Hark! ". . . in the deepest silence, only broken by the occasional flap of a sail, and the steady hum of the unceasingly advancing keel . . . 'Hist! Did you hear that noise . . . There it is again—under the hatches—don't you hear it—a cough—it sounded like a cough . . . There again—there it is!—it sounds like two or three sleepers turning over' . . . 'It's the three soaked biscuits ye eat for

supper turning over inside ye—nothing else . . . you are the chap, ain't ye, that heard the hum of the old Quakeress's knitting-needles fifty miles at sea from Nantucket' . . . 'Grin away; we'll see what turns up . . . there is somebody down in the after-hold that has not yet been seen on deck.'"

74 Chapter XLIV: The Chart. ". . . For with the charts of all four oceans before him, Ahab was threading a maze of currents and eddies . . . it might seem an absurdly hopeless task thus to seek out one solitary creature in the unhooped oceans of this planet. But not so did it seem to Ahab, who knew the sets of all tides and currents; and thereby calculating the driftings of the Sperm Whale's food . . . many hunters believe that . . . were the logs for one voyage of the entire whale fleet carefully collated, then the migrations of the Sperm Whale would be found to correspond in invariability to those of the herring-shoals or the flights of swallows . . . He sleeps with clenched hands; and wakes with his own bloody nails in his palms."

75 Chapter XLV: The Affidavit. ". . . not one in fifty of the actual disasters and deaths by casualties in the fishery, ever finds a public record at home . . . In the year 1820 the ship Essex . . . was cruising in the Pacific Ocean . . . suddenly, a very large whale escaping from the boats, issued from the shoal, and bore directly down upon the ship. Dashing his forehead against her hull, he so stove her in, that in less than "ten minutes" she settled down and fell over . . . there have been examples where the lines attached to a running Sperm Whale have, in a calm, been transferred to the ship, and secured there; the whale towing her great hull through the water, as a horse walks off with a cart . . . nor is it without conveying some eloquent indication of his character, that upon being attacked he will frequently open his mouth, and retain it in that dread expansion for several consecutive minutes . . . a great sea monster . . ."

76 Chapter XLVI: Surmises. ". . . Ahab in all his thoughts and actions ever had in view the ultimate capture of Moby Dick . . . I will not strip these men, thought Ahab, of all hopes of cash—aye, cash . . . Ahab plainly saw that he must still in a good degree continue true to the natural, nominal purpose of the Pequod's voyage . . . his voice was now often heard hailing the three mast-heads and admonishing them to keep a bright look-out, and not omit reporting even a porpoise."

77 Chapter XLVII: The Mat-Maker. "Queequeg and I were mildly employed weaving what is called a sword-mat . . . As I kept passing and repassing the filling or woof of marline between the long yarns of the warp, using my own hand for the shuttle, and as Queequeg, standing sideways, ever and anon slid his heavy oaken sword between the threads . . . it seemed as if this were the Loom of Time, and I myself were a shuttle mechanically weaving and weaving away at our Fates."

78 Chapter XLVII: The Mat-Maker. "'There she blows!' . . . The Sperm Whale blows as a clock ticks, with the same undeviating and reliable uniformity . . . 'There go flukes!' was now the cry from Tashtego; and the whales disappeared . . . The ship was now kept away from the wind, and she went gently rolling before it . . . But at this critical instant a sudden exclamation was heard that took every eye from the whale. With a start all glared at dark Ahab, who was surrounded by five dusky phantoms that seemed fresh formed out of air."

79 Chapter XLVII: The First Lowering. "The phantoms . . . were casting loose . . . one of the spare boats . . . the captain's . . . Ahab cried out to the white-turbaned old man at their head, 'All ready there, Fedallah?' . . . the three boats dropped into the sea . . . when a fourth keel, coming from the windward side, pulled round under stern, and showed

the five strangers rowing Ahab . . . I silently recalled the mysterious shadows I had seen creeping on board the Pequod during the dim Nantucket dawn . . ."

80 Chapter XLVII: The First Lowering. ". . . Starbuck said: "Stand up!' and Queequeg, harpoon in hand, sprang to his feet . . . A short rushing sound leaped out of the boat; it was the darted iron of Queequeg. Then all in one welded commotion came an invisible push from astern . . . Squall, whale, and harpoon had all blended together; and the whale, merely grazed by the iron, escaped . . . Though completely swamped, the boat was nearly unharmed . . . The wind increased to a howl; the waves dashed their bucklers together; the whole squall roared . . . Wet, drenched through, and shivering cold, despairing of ship or boat, we lifted up our eyes as the dawn came on. The mist still spread over the sea . . ."

81 Chapter XLVII: The First Lowering. "The sound came nearer and nearer; the thick mists were dimly parted by a huge, vague form. Affrighted, we all sprang into the sea as the ship at last loomed into view, bearing right down upon us within a distance of not much more than its length . . . we swam for it, were dashed against it by the seas, and were at last taken up and safely landed on board . . . This ship had given us up, but was still cruising, if haply it might light upon some token of our perishing . . ."

82 Chapter XLIX: The Hyena. "There are certain queer times and occasions in this strange mixed affair we call life when a man takes this whole universe for a vast practical joke . . . when they had dragged me, the last man, to the deck . . . 'Queequeg, my fine friend, does this sort of thing often happen?' . . . he gave me to understand that such things did often happen . . . 'Mr. Stubb,' said I . . . 'going plump on a flying whale with your sail set in a foggy squall is the height of a whaleman's discretion?' 'Certain.'

. . . said I . . . 'tell me whether it is an unalterable law in this fishery, Mr. Flask, for an oarsman to break his own back pulling himself back-first into death's jaws?' 'Yes, that's the law.' . . . from three impartial witnesses, I had a deliberate statement of the entire case . . . taking all things together, I saw, I thought I might as well go below and make a rough draft of my will."

83 Chapter L: Ahab's Boat and Crew, Fedallah. "Among whale-wise people it has often been argued whether, considering the paramount importance of his life to the success of the voyage, it is right for a whaling captain to jeopardize that life in the active perils of the chase . . . under these circumstances is it wise for any maimed man to enter a whaleboat in the hunt? As a general thing, the joint-owners of the Pequod must have plainly thought not . . . Therefor he had not solicited a boat's crew from them, nor had he in any way hinted his desires on that head. Nevertheless he had taken private measures of his own touching all that matter."

84 Chapter LI: The Spirit Spout. ". . . on such a silent night a silvery jet was seen far in advance of the white bubbles at the bow . . . for several successive nights without uttering a single sound; when, after all this silence, his unearthly voice was heard announcing that silvery, moon-lit jet . . . though the ship so swiftly sped . . . the silver jet was no more seen that night . . . Mysteriously jetted into the clear moonlight, or starlight, as the case may be; disappearing again for one whole day, or two days, or three; and somehow seeming at every distinct repetition to be advancing still further and further in our van, this solitary jet seemed for ever alluring us on . . . some of the seamen who swore . . . that unnearable spout was cast by . . . Moby Dick . . . as if it were treacherously beckoning us on and on, in order that the mon-

ster might turn round upon us, and rend us at last in the remotest and most savage seas."

85 Chapter LII: The Albatross. ". . . a sail loomed ahead, the Goney (Albatross) by name . . . had survived nearly four years of cruising . . . a Nantucketer and shortly bound home, [Ahab] loudly hailed—"Ahoy there! This is the Pequod, bound round the world! Tell them to address all future letters to the Pacific Ocean!"

86 Chapter LIII: The Gam. "For the long absent ship, the out-ward-bounder, perhaps, has letters on board; at any rate, she will be sure to let her have some papers of a date a year or two later than the last one on her blurred and thumb-worn files. And in return for that courtesy, the out-ward-bound ship would receive the latest whaling intel-ligence from the cruising-ground to which she may be destined . . . She has a 'gam' . . . GAM. Noun—*A social meeting of two (or more) Whale-ships, generally on a cruis-ing-ground; when, after exchanging hails, they exchange visits by boats' crews; the two captains remaining, for the time, on board of one ship, and the two chief mates on the other.*"

87 Chapter LIV: The Town-Ho Story. ". . . another home-ward-bound whaleman, the Town-Ho . . . interest in the White Whale was now wildly heightened by a circumstance of the Town-Ho's story . . . the order about the shovel was almost as plainly meant to sting and insult Steelkit, as though Radney had spat in his face . . . Steelkit, clench-ing his right hand behind him, and creepingly drawing it back, told his persecutor that if the hammer but grazed his cheek he (Steelkit) would murder him . . . the next instant the lower jaw of the mate was stove in his head; he fell on the hatch spouting blood . . . the valiant captain danced up and down with a whale-pike, calling upon his officers to manhandle that atrocious scoundrel . . . Steelkit and his

desperadoes were too much for them all; they succeeded in gaining the forecastle deck . . . entrenched themselves behind the barricade . . . (Steelkit's) death would be the signal for a murderous mutiny . . . Steelkit systematically built the plan of his revenge . . . a fool saved the would-be murderer from the bloody deed he had planned . . . all at once shouted . . . It was Moby Dick . . . Radney was tossed over into the sea . . . the whale rushed round in a sudden maelstrom; seized the swimmer between his jaws; and rearing high up with him, plunged headlong again, and went down."

88 Chapter LV: Of the Monstrous Pictures of Whales. "It is time to set the world right in this matter, by proving such pictures of the whale all wrong . . . looks more like the tapering tail of an anaconda, than the broad palms of the true whale's majestic flukes . . . the book-binder's whale winding like a vine-stalk round the stock of a descending anchor . . . the whales, like great rafts of logs, are represented lying among ice-isles, with white bears running over their living backs . . . Cuvier's Sperm Whale is not a Sperm Whale, but a squash . . . Richard III whales, with dromedary humps, and very savage . . . But these manifold mistakes in depicting the whale are not very surprising after all . . . Though elephants have stood for their full-lengths, the living Leviathan has never yet fairly floated himself for his portrait."

89 Chapter LVI: Of the Less Erroneous Pictures of Whales, and the True Pictures of Whaling Scenes. ". . . the finest . . . whaling scenes to be found anywhere, are two large French engravings . . . The French are the lads for painting action . . . as in that triumphed hall at Versailles . . . Not wholly unworthy of a place in that gallery, are these sea battle-pieces of Garnery . . . With not one tenth of England's experience in the fishery, and not the thou-

sandth part of that of the Americans, they have nevertheless furnished both nation with the only finished sketches
at all capable of conveying the real spirt of the whale hunt
. . . American whale draughtsmen seem entirely content
with presenting the mechanical outline of things . . . I
mean no disparagement to the excellent voyager . . ."

90 Chapter LVII: Of Whales in Paint; in Teeth; in Wood; in
Sheet-Iron; in Stone; in Mountains; in Stars. ". . . in Nantucket, and New Bedford, and Sag Harbor, you will come
across lively sketches of whales and whaling-scenes,
graven by the fishermen themselves on Sperm Whale
teeth . . . and other skrimshander articles, as the whalemen call the numerous little contrivances they elaborately
carve out of the rough material . . . Wooden whales, or
whales cut in profile out of the small dark slabs of the
noble South Sea war-wood, are frequently met with in the
forecastles of American whalers . . . At some old gable-
roofed country houses you will see brass whales hung by
the tail for knockers on the road-side door . . . On the
spires of some old-fashioned churches you will see sheet-
iron whales placed there for weathercocks . . ."

91 Chapter LVIII: Brit. ". . . we fell in with vast meadows of brit,
the minute, yellow substance upon which the Right Whale
largely feeds . . . we know the sea to be an everlasting terra
incognita . . . That same ocean rolls now; that same ocean
destroyed the wrecked ships of last year. Yea, foolish mortals, Noah's flood is not yet subsided, two thirds of the fair
world it yet covers . . . then turn to this green, gentle, and
most docile earth . . . on in the soul of man there lies one
insular Tahiti, full of peace and joy, but encompassed by all
the horrors of the half known life. God keep thee! Push not
off from that isle, thou canst never return!"

92 Chapter LIX: Squid. "In the distance, a great white mass
lazily rose . . . 'the White Whale!'" . . . The four boats were

soon on the water; Ahab's in advance, and all swiftly pulling towards their prey . . . once more it slowly rose . . . A
vast pulpy mass, furlongs in length and breadth . . . 'The
great live Squid' . . . they believe it to furnish to the Sperm
Whale his only food."

93 Chapter LX: The Line. ". . . I have here to speak of the
magical sometimes horrible whale-line . . . measures
something over two-hundred fathoms. Towards the stern
of the boat it is spirally coiled away in the tub . . . when thus
hung in hangman's nooses . . . the six men composing the
crew pull into the jaws of death, with a halter around every
neck, as you may say . . . when the line is darting out, to be
seated then in the boat, is like being seated in the midst of
the manifold whizzings of a steam-engine in full play . . ."

94 Chapter LXI: Stubb Kills a Whale. "And lo! close under our
lee, not forty fathoms off, a gigantic Sperm Whale lay rolling in the water like the capsized hull of a frigate . . . ere the
boats were down, majestically turning, [the whale] swam
away to the leeward . . . 'Stand up, Tashtego!—give it to
him!' The harpoon was hurled . . . 'Haul in—haul in!' cried
Stubb to the bowsman! and, facing round towards the
whale, all hands began pulling the boat up to him, while yet
the boat was being towed on. Soon ranging up by his flank,
Stubb, firmly planting his knee in the clumsy cleat, darted
dart after dart into the flying fish . . . At last, gush after gush
of clotted red gore, as if it had been the purple lees of red
wine, shot into the frighted air; and falling back again, ran
dripping down his motionless flanks into the sea. His heart
had burst! . . . Stubb . . . for a moment, stood thoughtfully
eyeing the vast corpse he had made."

95 Chapter LXII: The Dart. "Now it needs a strong, nervous
arm to strike the first iron into the fish; for often, in what
is called a long dart, the heavy implement has to be flung
to the distance of twenty or thirty feet . . . No wonder, tak-

ing the whole fleet of whalemen in a body, that out of fifty fair chances for a dart, not five are successful; no wonder that so many hapless harpooners are madly cursed and disrated . . . for it is the harpooner that makes the voyage."

96 Chapter LXIII: The Crotch. "It is customary to have two harpoons reposing in the crotch, respectively called the first and second irons. But these two harpoons each by its own cord, are both connected with the line; the object being this: to dart them both, if possible, one instantly after the other into the same whale; so that if, in the coming drag, one should draw out, the other may still retain a hold. It is a doubling of chances. But it very often happens that owing to the instantaneous, violent, convulsive running of the whale upon receiving the first iron, it becomes impossible for the harpooner, however lightning-like in his movements, to pitch the second iron into him . . . when the second iron is thrown overboard, it thenceforth becomes a dangling, sharp-edged terror, skittishly curvetting about both boat and whale, entangling the lines, or cutting them, and making a prodigious sensation in all directions. Nor, in general, is it possible to secure it again until the whale is fairly captured and a corpse."

97 Chapter LXIV: Stubb's Supper. "Tied by the head to the stern and by the tail to the bows, the whale now lies with its black hull close to the vessel's . . . Stubb was a high liver; he was somewhat intemperately fond of the whale as a flavorish thing to his palate . . . About midnight that steak was cut and cooked . . . Mingling their mumblings with [Stubb's] own mastications, thousands on thousands of sharks, swarming round the dead Leviathan, smackingly feasted on its fatness . . . 'Cook,' said Stubb, rapidly lifting a rather reddish morsel to his mouth, 'don't you think this steak is rather overdone? . . . There are those sharks now over the side, don't you see they prefer it tough and rare?'

. . . 'Wish by Gor! whale eat him, 'stead of him eat whale, I'm bressed if he ain't more of shark dan Massa Shark hisself,' muttered the old man."

98 Chapter LXV: The Whale as a Dish. "That mortal man should feed upon the creature that feeds his lamp, and, like Stubb, eat him by his own light, as you may say; this seems so outlandish a thing . . . the whale would by all hands be considered a noble dish, were there not so much of him; but when you come to sit down before a meat-pie nearly one hundred feet long, it takes away your appetitie . . . what further deprecates the whale as a civilized dish, his exceeding richness . . . Go to the meat-market of a Saturday night and see the crowds of live bipeds staring up at the long rows of dead quadrupeds. Does not that sight take a tooth out of the cannibal's jaw? Cannibals? who is not a cannibal?"

99 Chapter LXVI: The Shark Massacre. ". . . Queequeg and a forecastle seaman came on deck . . . and lowering three lanterns, so that they cast long gleams of light over the turbid sea, these two mariners, darting their long whaling-spades, kept up an incessant murdering of the sharks, by striking the keen steel deep into their skulls . . . the marksmen could not always hit their mark . . . [The sharks] viciously snapped, not only at each other's disembowelments, but like flexible bows, bent round, and bit their own; till those entrails seemed swallowed over and over again by the same mouth . . ."

100 Chapter LXVII: Cutting In. "The ivory Pequod was turned into what seemed a shamble; every sailor a butcher. You would have thought we were offering up ten thousand red oxen to the sea gods . . . to this block the great blubber hook, weighing some one hundred pounds, was attached . . . the hook is inserted, and the main body of the crew striking up a wild chorus, now commence heaving in one

dense crowd at the windlass. When instantly, the entire ship careens over on her side . . . at last, a swift, startling snap is heard; with a great swash the ship rolls upwards and backwards from the whale, and the triumphant tackle rises into sight dragging after it the disengaged semicircular end of the first strip of blubber . . ."

101 Chapter LXVIII: The Blanket. "For the whale is indeed wrapt up in his blubber as in a real blanket . . . the whale is enabled to keep himself comfortable in all weathers, in all seas . . . that warm themselves under the lee of an iceberg . . . Do thou, too, remain warm among ice . . . Be cool at the equator, keep they blood fluid at the Pole."

102 Chapter LXIX: The Funeral. ". . . 'Let the carcase go astern!' . . . The vast white headless phantom floats further and further from the ship . . . The sea-vultures all in pious mourning, the air-sharks all punctiliously in black or speckled . . . Espied by some timid man-of-war or blundering discovery-vessel from afar . . . with trembling fingers is set down in the log —*shoals, rocks, and breakers hereabouts: beware!* And for years afterwards, perhaps, ships shun the place . . ."

103 Chapter LXX: The Sphynx. ". . . previous to completely stripping the body of the Leviathan, he was beheaded. Now, the beheading of the Sperm Whale is a scientific anatomical feat . . . for the Sperm Whale's head embraces nearly one third of his entire bulk . . . It was a black and hooded head; and hanging there in the midst of so intense a calm, it seemed the Sphynx's in the desert. 'Speak, thou vast and venerable head,' muttered Ahab."

104 Chapter LXXI: The Jeroboam's Story. "Squaring her yards, she bore down, ranged abeam under the Pequod's lee, and lowered a boat . . . Pulling an oar in the Jeroboam's boat, was a man of singular appearance . . . He had been

originally nurtured among the crazy society of Neskyeuna Shakers . . . upon the ship's getting out of sight of land, his insanity broke out in a freshet. He announced himself as the archangel Gabriel and commanded the captain to jump overboard . . . all the preternatural terrors of real delirium, united to invest this Gabriel in the minds of the majority of the ignorant crew, with an atmosphere of sacredness. Moreover, they were afraid of him. As such a man, however, was not of much practical use in the ship, especially as he refused to work except when he pleased . . . So strongly did he work upon his disciples among the crew, that at last in a body they went to the captain and told him if Gabriel was sent from the ship, not a man of them would remain . . . it came to pass that Gabriel had the complete freedom of the ship . . . The sailors, mostly poor devils, cringed, and some of them fawned before him; in obedience to his instructions, sometimes rendering him personal homage, as to a god. Such things may seem incredible; but, however wondrous, they are true."

105 Chapter LXXII: The Monkey-Rope. "We must now retrace our way a little. It was mentioned that upon first breaking ground in the whale's back, the blubber-hook was inserted . . . But how did so clumsy and weighty a mass as that same hook get fixed in that hole? It was inserted there by my particular friend Queequeg, whose duty it was, as harpooner, to descend upon the monster's back . . . But in very many cases, circumstances require that the harpooner shall remain on the whale till the whole flensing or stripping operation is concluded . . . the vast mass revolves like a tread-mill beneath him . . . it was my cheerful duty to attend upon him while taking that hard-scrabble scramble upon the dead whale's back . . . from the ship's side, did I hold Queequeg down there in the sea, by what is technically called in the fishery a monkey-rope, attached to a strong strip of canvas belted round his waist."

Appendix

106 Chapter LXXIII: Stubb and Flask Kill a Right Whale; and Then Have a Talk Over Him. ". . . now that a Sperm Whale had been brought alongside and beheaded, to the surprise of all, the announcement was made that a Right Whale should be captured that day, if opportunity offered. Nor was this long wanting. Tall spouts were seen to leeward; and two boats, Stubb's and Flask's, were detached in pursuit . . . At last his spout grew thick, and with a frightful roll and vomit, he turned upon his back a corpse . . . 'did you never hear that the ship which but once has a Sperm Whale's head hoisted on her starboard side, and at the same time a Right Whale's on the larboard; did you never hear, Stubb, that that ship can never afterwards capsize? . . . I heard that gamboge ghost of a Fedallah saying so, and he seems to know all about ships' charms.' . . . 'I take that Fedallah to be the devil in disguise . . . The reason why you don't see his tail, is because he tucks it up out of sight' . . ."

107 Chapter LXXIV: The Sperm Whale's Head—Contrasted View. "Now, from this peculiar sideway position of the whale's eyes, it is plain that he can never see an object which is exactly ahead, no more than he can one exactly astern . . . There are generally forty-two teeth in all; in old whales, much worn down, but undecayed; nor filled after our artificial fashion. The jaw is afterwards sawn into slabs, and piled away like joists for building houses." Chapter LXXV: The Right Whale's Head—Contrasted View. "As in general shape the noble Sperm Whale's head may be compared to a Roman war-chariot (especially in front where it is so broadly rounded) . . ."

108 Chapter LXXV: The Right Whale's Head—Contrasted View. ". . . at a broad view, the Right Whale's head bears a rather inelegant resemblance to a gigantic galliot-toed shoe. Two hundred years ago an old Dutch voyager likened its shape

to that of a shoemaker's last . . . fix your eye upon this strange, crested, comb-like incrustation of the top of the mass—this green, barnacled thing, which the Greenlanders call the 'crown' . . . we now slide into the mouth . . . The roof is about twelve feet high, and runs to a pretty sharp angle . . . these ribbed, arched, hairy sides, present us with those wondrous, half vertical scimitar-shaped slats of whalebone . . . for those Ventian blinds which have elsewhere been cursorily mentioned . . . through which the Right Whale strains the water, and in whose intricacies he retains small fish, when open-mouthed he goes through the seas of brit in feeding time."

109 Chapter LXXVI: The Battering-Ram. ". . . intelligent estimate of whatever battering-ram power may be lodged there . . . the front of the Sperm Whale's head is a dead, blind wall, without a single organ or tender prominence of any sort whatsoever . . . and not till you get twenty feet from the forehead do you come to the full cranial development. So that this whole enormous boneless mass is as one wad. Finally, though, as will soon be revealed, its contents partly comprise the most delicate oil . . . The severest pointed harpoon, the sharpest lance darted by the strongest human arm, impotently rebounds from it . . . and be ready to abide by this; that though the Sperm Whale stove a passage through the Isthmus of Darien, and mixed the Atlantic with the Pacific, you would not elevate one hair of your eye-brow."

110 Chapter LXXVII: The Great Heidelburgh Tun. "Now comes the Baling of the Case. But to comprehend it aright, you must know something of the curious internal structure of the thing operated upon. Regarding the Sperm Whale's head . . . The upper part, known as the Case, may be regarded as the great Heidelburgh Tun of the Sperm Whale . . . contains by far the most precious of all his oily vintages;

namely, the highly-prized spermaceti . . . Though in life it remains perfectly fluid, yet, upon exposure to the air, after death, it soon begins to concrete; sending forth beautiful crystalline shoots . . . A large whale's case generally yields about five hundred gallons of sperm, though from unavoidable circumstances, considerable of it is spilled, leaks, and dribbles away, or is otherwise irrevocably lost in the ticklish business of securing what you can."

111 Chapter LXXVIII: Cistern and Bucket. "Nimble as a cat, Tashtego mounts aloft . . . to the part where it exactly projects over the hoisted Tun . . . he diligently searches for the proper place to begin breaking into the Tun . . . Tashtego downward guides the bucket into the Tun, till it entirely disappears . . . up comes the bucket again, all bubbling like a dairy-maid's pail of new milk . . . several tubs had been filled with the fragrant sperm; when all at once a queer accident happened . . . my God! poor Tashtego—like the twin reciprocating bucket in a veritable well, dropped head-foremost down into this great Tun of Heidelburgh, and with a horrible oily gurgling, went clean out of sight! . . . a sharp cracking noise was heard; and to the unspeakable horror of all, one of the two enormous hooks suspending the head tore out . . . with a thunder-boom, the enormous mass dropped into the sea . . . while poor, buried-alive Tashtego was sinking utterly down to the bottom of the sea! . . . a loud splash announced that my brave Queequeg had dived to the rescue . . . soon after, Queequeg was seen boldly striking out with one hand, and with the other clutching the long hair of the Indian."

112 Chapter LXXIX: The Prairie. ". . . the Sperm Whale is an anomalous creature. He has no proper nose . . . Few are the foreheads which like Shakespeare's or Melancthon's rise so high, and descend so low, that the eyes themselves seem clear, eternal, tideless mountain lakes; and all above

them in the forehead's wrinkles, you seem to track the ant-lered thoughts descending there to drink . . . in the great Sperm Whale, this high and mighty god-like dignity inher-ent in the brow is so immensely amplified, that gazing on it, in that full front view, you feel the Deity and the dread powers more forcibly than in beholding any other object in living nature. For you see no one point precisely; not one distinct feature is revealed; no nose, eyes, ears, or mouth; no face; he has none, proper; nothing but that one broad firmament of a forehead . . . Nor in profile, does this won-drous brow diminish . . . But how? Genius in the Sperm Whale? Has the Sperm Whale ever written a book, spoken a speech? No, his great genius is declared in his doing nothing particular to prove it."

113 Chapter LXXX: The Nut. "In the full-grown creature the skull will measure at least twenty feet in length . . . in another cavity seldom exceeding ten inches in length and as many in depth—reposes the mere handful of this monster's brain. The brain is at least twenty feet from his apparent forehead in life . . . For I believe that much of a man's character will be found betokened in his backbone. I would rather feel your spine that your skull, whoever you are . . . And what is still more, for many feet after emerging from the brain's cavity, the spinal cord remains of an unde-creasing girth, almost equal to that of the brain."

114 Chapter LXXXI: The Pequod Meets the Virgin. ". . . we duly met the ship Jungfrau . . . However curious it may seem for an oil-ship to be borrowing oil on the whale-ground . . . sometimes such a thing really happens; and in the present case Captain Derick De Deer did indubita-bly conduct a lamp-feeder as Flask did declare . . . not a single flying-fish yet captured to supply the deficiency . . . hinting that his ship was indeed . . . a clean one (that is, an empty one) . . . Derick departed; but he had not gained

his ship's side, when whales were almost simultaneously raised from the mast-heads of both vessels . . . many fathoms in the rear, swam a huge, humped old bull . . . all the combined rival boats were pointed for this one fish . . . Queequeg, Tashtego, Daggoo—instinctively sprang to their feet, and standing in a diagonal row, simultaneously pointed their barbs; and darted over the head of the German harpooner, their three Nantucket irons entered the whale . . . while the crews were awaiting the arrival of the ship, the body showed symptoms of sinking . . . With a terrific snap, every fastening went adrift; the ship righted; the carcase sank."

115 Chapter LXXXII: The Honor and Glory of Whaling. "The more I dive into this matter of whaling . . . the more I am impressed with its great honorableness and antiquity; and especially when I find so many great demi-gods and heroes . . . The gallant Perseus, a son of Jupiter, was the first whaleman . . . that famous story of St. George and the Dragon; which dragon I maintain to have been a whale . . . Hercules . . . that brawny doer of rejoicing good deeds, was swallowed down and thrown up by a whale . . . he may be deemed a sort of involuntary whaleman . . . derived from the still more ancient Hebrew story of Jonah and the whale . . . Vishnoo became incarnate in a whale, and sounding down in him to the uttermost depths, rescued the sacred volumes . . . Perseus, St. George, Hercules, Jonah, and Vishnoo! there's a member-roll for you!"

116 Citation lost!

117 Chapter LXXXIII: Jonah Historically Regarded. "Now some Nantucketers rather distrust this historical story of Jonah and the whale . . . consider Jonah as tombed in the whale's belly, but as temporarily lodged in some part

of his mouth . . . the Right Whale's mouth would accommodate a couple of whist-tables, and comfortably seat all the players . . . if I remember right: Jonah was swallowed by the whale in the Mediterranean Sea, and after three days he was vomited up somewhere within three days' journey of Ninevah, a city on the Tigris, very much more than three days' journey across from the nearest point of the Meditteranean coast . . . He might have carried him round by the way of the Cape of Good Hope . . . such a supposition would involve the complete circumnavigation of all Africa in three days . . ."

118 Chapter LXXXIV: Pitchpoling. ". . . none exceed that fine manoeuver with the lance called pitchpoling . . . Steel and wood included, the entire spear is some ten or twelve feet in length . . . Look now at Stubb . . . with a rapid, nameless impulse, in a superb lofty arch the bright steel spans the foaming distance, and quivers in the life spot of the whale. Instead of sparkling water, he now spouts red blood . . . Again and again to such gamesome talk, the dexterous dart is repeated, the spear returning to its master like a greyhound held in skillful leash. The agonized whale goes into his flurry; the towline is slackened, and the pitchpoler dropping astern, folds his hands, and mutely watches the monster die."

119 Chapter LXXXV: The Fountain. ". . . the whale, who systematically lives, by intervals, his full hour and more (when at the bottom) without drawing a single breath . . . among whalemen, the spout is deemed poisonous; they try to evade it. Another thing; I have heard it said, and I do not much doubt it, that if the jet is fairly spouted into your eyes, it will blind you . . . And I am convinced that from the heads of all ponderous profound beings, such as Plato, Pyrrho, the Devil, Jupiter, Dante, and so on, there always goes up a certain semi-visible steam, while in the act of

thinking deep thoughts. While composing a little treatise on Eternity, I had the curiosity to place a mirror before me; and ere long saw reflected there, a curious involved worming and undulation in the atmosphere over my head. The invariable moisture of my hair, while plunged in deep thought, after six cups of hot tea in my thin shingled attic, of an August noon; this seems an additional argument for the above supposition."

120 Chapter LXXXVI: The Tail. "Five great motions are peculiar to it. First, when used as a fin for progression; Second, when used as a mace in battle; Third, in sweeping; Fourth, in lobtailing; Fifth, in peaking flukes . . . First . . . It never wriggles. In man or fish, wriggling is a sign of inferiority . . . coiled forwards beneath the body, and then rapidly sprung backwards . . . Second . . . In striking at a boat, he swiftly curves away his flukes from it, and the blow is inflicted only by the recoil . . . Third . . . when in maidenly gentleness the whale with a certain soft slowness moves his immense flukes from side to side upon the surface of the sea . . . Fourth . . . The broad palms of his tail are flirted high into the air; then smiting the surface, the thunderous concussion resounds for miles . . . Fifth . . . when he is about to plunge into the deeps, his entire flukes with at least thirty feet of his body are tossed erect in the air, and so remain vibrating a moment, till they downwards shoot out of view."

121 Chapter LXXXVII: The Grand Armada. "Those narrow straits of Sunda divide Sumatra from Java . . . the piratical proas of the Malays, lurking among the low shaded coves and islets of Sumatra, have sallied out upon the vessels sailing through the straits . . . With a fair, fresh wind, the Pequod was now drawing nigh to these straits . . . Seen from the Pequod's deck, then, as she would rise on a high hill of the sea, this host of vapory spouts, individually curling up into the air . . . Crowding all sail

the Pequod pressed after them . . . the voice of Tashtego was heard, loudly directing attention to something in our wake . . . Levelling his glass at this sight, Ahab quickly revolved in his pivot-hole, crying, 'Aloft there, and rig whips and buckets to wet the sails;—Malays, sir, and after us!' . . . Ahab to-and-fro paced the deck; in his forward turn beholding the monsters he chased, and in the after one the bloodthirsty pirates chasing *him* . . . But thoughts like these troubled very few of the reckless crew; and when, after steadily dropping and dropping the pirates astern . . ."

122 Chapter LXXXVII: The Grand Armada. ". . . word was passed to spring to the boats. But no sooner did the herd, by some presumed wonderful instinct of the Sperm Whale, become notified of the three keels that were after them . . . moved on with redoubled velocity . . . after several hours' pulling were almost disposed to renounce the chase, when a general pausing commotion among the whales . . . In all directions expanding in vast irregular circles, and aimlessly swimming hither and thither, by their short thick spoutings, they plainly betrayed their distraction of panic . . . Queequeg's harpoon was flung; the stricken fish darted blinding spray in our faces, and then running away with us like light, steered straight for the heart of the herd . . . As, blind and deaf, the whale plunged forward, as if by sheer power of speed to rid himself of the iron leech that had fastened to him; as we thus tore a white gash in the sea . . ."

123 Chapter LXXXVII: The Grand Armada. "All whale-boats carry certain curious contrivances, originally invented by the Nantucket Indians, called druggs . . . It is chiefly among gallied whales that this drugg is used. For then, more whales are close round you than you can possibly chase at one time. But Sperm Whales are not every day encoun-

tered; while you may, then, you must kill all you can. And if you cannot kill them all at once, you must wing them, so that they can be afterwards killed at your leisure . . . The first and second were successfully darted, and we saw the whales staggeringly running off, fettered by the enormous sidelong resistance of the towing drugg . . . The result of this lowering was somewhat illustrative of that sagacious saying in the Fishery,—the more whales the less fish. Of all the drugged whales only one was captured."

124 Chapter LXXXVII: The Grand Armada. ". . . the jerking harpoon drew out, and the towing whale sideways vanished . . . In this central expanse the sea presented that smooth satin-like surface, called a sleek, produced by the subtle moisture thrown off by the whale in his more quiet moods . . . Keeping at the centre of the lake, we were occasionally visited by small tame cows and calves; the women and children of this routed host . . . Like household dogs they came snuffling round us, right up to our gunwales, and touching them; till it almost seemed that some spell had suddenly domesticated them. Queequeg patted their foreheads; Starbuck scratched their backs with his lance . . ."

125 Chapter LXXXVIII: Schools and Schoolmasters. "Such bands are known as schools. They generally are of two sorts; those composed almost entirely of females, and those mustering none but young vigorous males, or bulls, as they are familiarly designated. In cavalier attendance upon the school of females, you invariably see a male of full grown magnitude, but not old; who, upon any alarm, evinces his gallantry by falling in the rear and covering the flight of his ladies. In truth, this gentleman is a luxurious Ottoman, swimming about over the watery world, surroundingly accompanied by all the solaces and endearments of the harem . . . As ashore, the ladies often cause

the most terrible duels among their rival admirers; just so with the whales, who sometimes come to deadly battle, and all for love. They fence with their long lower jaws, sometimes locking them together, and so striving for the supremacy like elks that warringly interweave their antlers."

126 Chapter LXXXIX: Fast-Fish and Loose-Fish. "It frequently happens that when several ships are cruising in company, a whale may be struck by one vessel, then escape, and be finally killed and captured by another vessel . . . Thus the most vexations and violent disputes would often arise between the fishermen, were there not some written or unwritten, universal, undisputed law applicable to all cases . . . I. A Fast-Fish belongs to the party fast to it. II. A Loose-Fish is fair game for anybody who can sooner catch it . . . Alive or dead a fish is technically fast, when it is connected with an occupied ship or boat, by any medium at all controllable by the occupant or occupants,—a mast, an oar, a nine-inch cable, a telegraph wire, or a strand of cobweb, it is all the same . . . though the gentleman had originally harpooned her; yet abandoned the lady, and had once had her fast . . . had at last abandoned her; yet abandon her he did, so that she became a loose-fish . . . What was America 1492 but a Loose-Fish . . . What are the Rights of Man and the Liberties of the World but Loose-Fish? What all men's minds and opinions but Loose-Fish? . . . What is the great globe itself but a Loose-Fish?"

127 Chapter XC: Heads of Tails. ". . . the Laws of England, which taken along with the context, means, that of all whales captured by anybody on the coast of that land, the King, as Honorary Grand Harpooner, must have the head, and the Queen be respectfully presented with the tail. A division which, in the whale, is much like halving an apple; there is no intermediate remainder . . . But is the Queen a

mermaid, to be presented with a tail? An allegorical meaning may lurk here . . . the King receiving the highly dense and elastic head peculiar to that fish, which, symbolically regarded, may possibly be humorously grounded upon some presumed congeniality. And thus there seems a reason in all things, even in law."

128 Chapter XCI: The Pequod Meets the Rosebud. "Coming still nearer with the expiring breeze, we saw that the Frenchman had a second whale alongside; and this second whale seemed even more of a nosegay than the first. In truth, it turned out to be one of those problematical whales that seem to dry up and die with a sort of prodigious dyspepsia, or indigestion; leaving their defunct bodies almost entirely bankrupt of anything like oil . . . 'now that I think of it, it may contain something worth a good deal more than oil; yes, ambergris. I wonder now if our old man has thought of that. It's worth trying' . . . By this time Stubb was over the side, and getting into his boat, hailed the Guernsey-man to this effect,—that having a long towline in his boat, he would do what he could to help them, by pulling out the lighter whale of the two from the ship's side . . . Dropping his spade, [Stubb] thrust both hands in, and drew out handfuls of something that looked like ripe Windsor soap . . . And this, good friends, is ambergris . . ."

129 Chapter XCII: Ambergris. ". . . ambergris is soft, waxy, and so highly fragrant and spicy, that it is largely used in perfumery . . . Who would think, then, that such fine ladies and gentlemen should regale themselves with an essence found in the inglorious bowels of a sick whale! Yet so it is. By some, ambergris is supposed to be the cause, and by others the effect, of the dyspepsia in the whale."

130 Chapter XCIII: The Castaway. ". . . Stubb's after-oarsman chanced so to sprain his hand, as for a time to become quite maimed; and, temporarily, Pip was put into his place

. . . Now upon the second lowering, the boat paddled upon the whale; and as the fish received the darted iron, it gave its customary rap, which happened, in this instance, to be right under poor Pip's seat. The involuntary consternation of the moment caused him to leap, paddle in hand, out of the boat; and in such a way, that part of the slack whale line coming against his chest, he breasted it overboard with him, so as to become entangled in it, when at last plumping into the water . . . 'Damn him, cut!' roared Stubb; and so the whale was lost and Pip was saved . . . But we are all in the hands of the Gods; and Pip jumped again. It was under very similar circumstances to the first performance; but this time he did not breast out the line; and hence, when the whale started to run, Pip was left behind on the sea . . . By the merest chance the ship itself at last rescued him . . ."

131 Chapter XCIV: A Squeeze of the Hand. "As I sat there at my ease, cross-legged on the deck . . . I squeezed that sperm till I myself almost melted into it . . . I found myself unwittingly squeezing my co-laborers' hands in it, mistaking their hands for gentle globules. Such an abounding, affectionate, friendly, loving feeling did this avocation beget; that at last I was continually squeezing their hands, and looking up into their eyes sentimentally . . . descend into the blubber-room, and have a long talk with its inmates. This place has previously been mentioned as the receptacle for the blanket-pieces, when strip and hoisted from the whale . . . the gaffman hooks on to a sheet of blubber, and strives to hold it from slipping, as the ship pitches and lurches about. Meanwhile, the spademan stands on the sheet itself, perpendicularly chopping it into the portable horse-pieces. This space is sharp as hone can make it; the spademan's feet are shoeless . . . Toes are scarce among veteran blubber-room men."

Appendix

132 Chapter XCV: The Cassock. ". . . a glimpse of that unaccountable cone,—longer than a Kentuckian is tall, nigh a foot in diameter at the base, and jet-black as Yojo, the ebony idol of Queequeg. And an idol, indeed, it is; or, rather, in old times, its likeness was. Such an idol as that found in the secret groves of Queen Maachah in Judea . . . Look at the sailor, called the mincer, who now comes along . . . removing some three feet of it, towards the pointed extremity, and then cutting two slits for arm-holes at the other end, he lengthwise slips himself bodily into it."

133 Chapter XCVI: The Try-Works. ". . . an American whaler is outwardly distinguished by her try-works . . . It is as if from the open field a brick-kiln were transported to her planks . . . By midnight the works were in full operation. We were clear from the carcase; sail had been made; the wind was freshening; the wild ocean darkness was intense . . . To every pitch of the ship there was a pitch of the boiling oil, which seemed all eagerness to leap into their faces . . . as I stood at her helm . . . My God! what was the matter with me? thought I. Lo! in my brief sleep I had turned myself about, and was fronting the ship's stern, with my back to her prow and the compass. In an instant I faced back, just in time to prevent the vessel from flying up into the wind, and very probably capsizing her."

134 Chapter XCII: The Lamp. "In merchantmen, oil for the sailor is more scarce than the milk of queens. To dress in the dark, and eat in the dark, and stumble in the darkness to his pallet, this is his usual lot. But the whaleman, as he seeks the food of light, so he lives in the light. He makes his berth an Aladdin's lamp, and lays him down in it; so that in the pitchiest night the ship's black hull still houses an illumination."

135 Chapter XCVIII: Stowing Down and Clearing Up. "While still warm, the oil, like hot punch, is received into the

six-barrel casks; and while, perhaps the ship is pitching and rolling this way and that in the midnight sea, the enormous casks are slewed round and headed over, end for end, and sometimes perilously scoot across the slippery deck, like so many landslides, till at last man-handled and stayed in their course . . . Hands go diligently along the bulwarks, and with buckets of water and rags restore them to their full tidiness. The soot is brushed from the lower rigging. All the numerous implements which have been in use are likewise cleansed and put away. The great hatch is scrubbed . . . continuing straight through for ninety-six hours . . . when—*There she blows!*—the ghost is spouted up, and away we sail to fight some other world, and go through young life's old routine again."

136 Chapter XCIX: The Doubloon. ". . . the doubloon of the Pequod was a most wealthy example . . . you saw the likeness of three Andes' summits; from one a flame; a tower on another; on the third a crowing cock; while arching over all was a segment of the partitioned zodiac . . . Ahab . . . 'There's something ever egotistical in mountain-tops and towers, and all other grand and lofty things; look here,—three peaks as proud as Lucifer. The firm tower, that is Ahab; the volcano, that is Ahab; the courageous, the undaunted, and victorious fowl, that, too, is Ahab; all are Ahab . . . murmured Starbuck . . . 'A dark valley, between three mighty, heaven-abiding peaks, that almost seem the Trinity' . . . soliloquized Stubb . . . 'Look you, Doubloon, your zodiac here is the life of man in one round chapter' . . . 'I see nothing here, but a round thing made of gold . . . It is worth sixteen dollars . . . at two cents the cigar, that's nine hundred and sixty cigars . . . so here goes Flask aloft' . . . 'This way comes Pip' . . . 'And so they'll say in the resurrection, when they come to fish up this old mast, and find a doubloon lodged in it, with bedded oysters for the shaggy bark.'"

137 Ibid.

138 Chapter C: Leg and Arm. The Pequod, of Nantucket, Meets the Samuel Enderby, of London. ". . . hailing a ship showing English colors . . . 'Hast seen the White Whale?' 'See you this?' and withdrawing it from the folds that had hidden it, [the English captain] held up a white arm of Sperm Whale bone . . . 'Did'st thou cross his wake again?' 'Twice.' 'But could not fasten?' 'Didn't want to try; ain't one limb enough?' . . . "Bless my soul, and curse the foul fiend's,' cried Bunger [the English doctor], stoopingly walking round Ahab, and like a dog, strangely snuffing; 'this man's blood—bring the thermometer!—it's at the boiling point!—his pulse makes these planks beat—sir!'—taking a lancet from his pocket, and drawing near to Ahab's arm. 'Avast!' roared Ahab, dashing him against the bulwarks—'Man the boat! Which way heading?' 'Good god!' cried the English captain, to whom the question was put. 'What's the matter. He was heading east, I think—is your captain crazy?' whispering Fedallah."

139 Chapter CI: The Decanter. ". . . the late Samuel Enderby, merchant of that city, the original of the famous whaling house of Enderby & Sons . . . in that year (1775) it fitted out the first English ships that ever regularly hunted the Sperm Whale . . . In 1778, a fine ship, the Amelia, fitted out for the express purpose, and at the sole charge of the vigorous Enderbys, boldly rounded Cape Horn, and was the first among the nations to lower a whale-boat of any sort in the great South Sea . . . thus the vast Sperm Whale grounds of the Pacific were thrown open . . . Samuel Enderby, and some other English whalers I know of—not all though—were such famous, hospitable ships; that passed round the beef, and the bread, and the can, and the joke; and were not soon weary of eating, and drinking, and laughing? The English were preceeded in the whale fishery by the Hollanders, Zealanders, and Danes . . . their fat old

fashions, touching plenty to each and drink . . . beef . . .
Friesland pork . . . stock fish . . . biscuit . . . soft bread . . .
butter . . . cheese . . . beer . . . gin . . . Now, whether these
gin and beer harpooners, so fuddled as one might fancy
them to have been, were the right sort of men to stand
up in a boat's head, and take good aim at flying whales;
this would seem somewhat improbable. Yet they did aim at
them, and hit them too."

140 Chapter CII: A Bower in the Arsacides. "I confess, that
since Jonah, few whalemen have penetrated very far
beneath the skin of the adult whale; nevertheless, I have
been blessed with an opportunity to dissect him in min-
iature. In a ship I belonged to, a small cub Sperm Whale
was once bodily hoisted to the deck . . . Think you I let that
chance go, without using my boat-hatchet and jack-knife,
and breaking the seal and reading all the contents of that
young cub? As for my exact knowledge of the bones of
the Leviathan in their gigantic, full grown development, for
that rare knowledge I am indebted to my late royal friend
Tranquo, king of Tranque . . . the skeleton was carefully
transported up the Pupella glen, where a grand temple
of lordly palms now sheltered it . . . Cutting me a green
measuring-rod, I once more dived within the skeleton . . .
dimensions I shall now proceed to set down are copied
verbatim from my right arm, where I had them tattooed; as
in my wild wanderings at that period, there was no other
secure way of preserving such valuable statistics."

141 Chapter CIII: Measurements of the Whale's Skeleton. "In
length, the Sperm Whale's skeleton at Tranque measured
seventy-two feet; so that when fully invested and extended
in life, he must have been ninety feet long . . . Of this seventy-two feet, his skull and jaw comprised some twenty
feet, leaving some fifty feet of plain back-bone . . . The
ribs were ten on a side. The first, to begin from the neck,

was nearly six feet long; the second, third, and fourth were each successively longer, till you came to the climax of the fifth, or one of the middle ribs, which measured eight feet and some inches . . . There are forty and odd vertebrae . . . The smallest, where the spine tapers away into the tail, is only two inches in width, and looks something like a white-billiard-ball. I was told that there were still smaller ones, but they had been lost by some little cannibal urchins, the priest's children, who had stolen them to play marbles with. Thus we see that the spine of even the hugest of living things tapers off at last into simple child's play."

142 Chapter CIV: The Fossil Whale. "Detached broken fossils of pre-adamite whales, fragments of their bones and skeletons, have within thirty years past, at various intervals, been found . . . But by far the most wonderful of all cetacean relics was the almost complete vast skeleton of an extinct monster, found in the year 1842, on the plantation of Judge Creagh, in Alabama. The awe-stricken credulous slaves in the vicinity took it for the bones of one of the fallen angels. The Alabama doctors declared it a huge reptile, and bestowed upon it the name of Basilosaurus . . . Who can show a pedigree like Leviathan? Ahab's harpoon had shed older blood then the Pharaoh's."

143 Chapter CV: Does the Whale's Magnitude Diminish?—Will He Perish? ". . . the moot point is, whether Leviathan can long endure so wide a chase, and so remorseless a havoc; whether he must not at last be exterminated from the waters . . . Comparing the humped herds of whales with the humped herds of buffalo, which, not forty years ago, overspread by tens of thousands the prairies of Illinois and Missouri . . . in such a comparison an irresistible argument would seem furnished to show that the hunted whale cannot now escape speedy extinction . . . Forty men in one ship hunting the Sperm Whale for forty-eight months think

they have done extremely well, and thank God, if at last they carry home the oil of forty fish . . . the same number of moccasined men, for the same number of months, mounted on horse instead of sailing in ships, would have slain not forty, but forty thousand and more buffaloes . . . Nor, considered aright, does it seem any argument in favor of gradual extinction of the Sperm Whale, for example, that in former years (the latter part of the last century, say) these Leviathans, in small pods, were encountered much oftener than at present . . . But though for some time past a number of these whales, not less than 13,000, have been annually slain on the nor' west coast by the Americans alone . . . yet what shall we say to Harto, the historian of Goa, when he tells us that at one hunting the King of Siam took 4000 elephants; that in those regions elephants are numerous as droves of cattle in the temperate climes . . . if they still survive there in great numbers, much more may the great whale outlast all hunting, since he has pasture to expatiate in, which is precisely twice as large as all Asia, both Americas, Europe and Africa, New Holland, and all the Isles of the sea combined . . . for all these things, we account the whale immortal in his species, however perishable in his individuality."

144 Chapter CVI: Ahab's Leg. "The precipitating manner in which Captain Ahab had quitted the Samuel Enderby of London, had not been unattended with some small violence to his own person. He had lighted with such energy upon a thwart of his boat that his ivory leg had received a half-splintering shock . . . For it had not been very long prior to the Pequod's sailing from Nantucket, that he had been found one night lying prone upon the ground, and insensible; by some unknown, and seemingly inexplicable, unimaginable casualty, his ivory limb having been so violently displaced, that it had stake-wise smitten, and all but pierced his groin; nor was it without extreme difficulty that

the agonizing wound was entirely cured. Nor, at the time, had it failed to enter his monomaniac mind, that all the anguish of that then present suffering was but the direct issue of a former woe . . . concerning Ahab, always had it remained a mystery to some, why it was, that for a certain period, both before and after the sailing of the Pequod, he had hidden himself away with such Grand-Lama-like exclusiveness . . . That direful mishap was at the bottom of his temporary recluseness."

145 Chapter CVII: The Carpenter. ". . . ordinary duties:— repairing stove boats, sprung spars, reforming the shape of clumsy-bladed oars, inserting bull's eyes in the deck, or new tree-nails in the side plans, and other miscellaneous matters . . . A lost land-bird of strange plumage strays on board, and is made a captive: out of clean shaved rods of Right Whale bone, and cross-beams of Sperm Whale ivory, the carpenter makes a pagoda-looking cage for it . . . Stubb longed for vermillion stars to be painted upon the blade of his every oar . . . the carpenter symmetrically supplies the constellation . . . A sailor takes a fancy to wear shark-bone ear-rings: the carpenter drills his ears. Another has a toothache: the carpenter out pincers . . . draw the tooth . . . a common pocket knife . . . So, if his superiors wanted to use the carpenter for a screw-driver, all they had to do was to open that part of him, and the screw was fast: or if for tweezers, take him up by the legs, and there they were."

146 Chapter CVIII; Ahab and the Carpenter. "'Hold; while Prometheus is about it; I'll order a complete man after a desirable pattern. Imprimis, fifty feet high in his socks; then, chest modelled after the Thames Tunnel; then, legs with roots to 'em . . . shall I order eyes to see outwards? No, but put a sky-light on top of his head to illuminate inwards. There, take the order, and away . . . I shall nev-

ertheless feel another leg in the same identical place with it; that is, carpenter, my old lost leg; the flesh and blood one, I mean . . . And if I still feel the smart of my crushed leg, though it be now so long dissolved; then, why mayst not thou, carpenter, feel the fiery pains of hell for ever, and without a body? Hah!'"

147 Chapter CIX: Ahab and Starbuck in the Cabin. "According to usage they were pumping the ship next morning; and lo! no inconsiderable oil came up with the water; the casks below must have sprung a bad lead . . . Starbuck went down into the cabin to report this unfavorable affair . . . 'Captain Ahab . . . The oil in the hold is leaking, Sir. We must up Burtons and break out.' . . . 'Begone! Let it leak! I'm all aleak myself.' . . . 'Nay, Sir, not yet; I do entreat.' . . . Ahab seized a loaded musket from the rack . . . and pointing it toward Starbuck exclaimed: 'There is one God that is Lord over the earth, and one Captain that is lord over the Pequod.—On deck!' . . . 'let Ahab beware of Ahab; beware of thyself, old man.' 'What's that he said—Ahab beware of Ahab—there's something there! . . . Thou art but too good a fellow, Starbuck . . . up Burtons, and break out in the main-hold.'"

148 Chapter CX: Queequeg in His Coffin. "Poor Queequg! when the ship was about half disemboweled . . . the tattooed savage was crawling about amid that dampness and slime like a green spotted lizard at the bottom of a well . . . for all the heat of his sweatings, he caught a terrible chill which lapsed into a fever; and at last, after some days' suffering, laid him in his hammock, close to the very sill of the door of death . . . he shuddered at the thought of being buried in his hammock, according to the usual sea-custom . . . No: he desired a canoe like those of Nantucket . . . these coffin-canoes . . . the carpenter for convenience sake and general reference, now trans-

ferringly measured on it the exact length the coffin was to be, and then made the transfer permanent by cutting two notches at the extremities. This done, he marshalled the planks and his tools, and to work . . . When the last nail was driven . . . Queequeg, to every one's consternation, commanded that the thing should be instantly brought to him . . . He then called for his harpoon . . . and a piece of sail-cloth being rolled up for a pillow, Queequeg now entreated to be lifted into his final bed . . . He lay without moving a few minutes, then told one to go to his bag and bring out his little god, Yojo . . . he called for the coffin lid (hatch he called it) to be placed over him."

149 Chapter CX: Queequeg in His Coffin. "But now that he had apparently made every preparation for death; now that his coffin was proved a good fit, Queequeg suddenly rallied . . . the cause of his sudden convalescence was this;—at a critical moment, he had just recalled a little duty ashore, which he was leaving undone; and therefor had changed his mind about dying; he could not die yet, he averred . . . he suddenly leaped to his feet, threw out arms and legs, gave himself a good stretching, yawned a little bit, and then springing into the head of his hoisted boat, and poising a harpoon, pronounced himself fit for a fight. With a wild whimsiness, he now used his coffin for a sea-chest . . ."

150 Chapter CXI: The Pacific. "When gliding by the Bashee isles we emerged at last upon the great South Sea; were it not for other things, I could have greeted my dear Pacific with uncounted thanks . . . that serene ocean rolled eastwards from me a thousand leagues of blue. There is, one knows not what sweet mystery about this sea . . . Thus this mysterious, divine Pacific zones the world's whole bulk about; makes all coasts one bay to it; seems the tide-beating heart of earth . . . But few thoughts of Pan

stirred Ahab's brain, as standing like an iron statue at his accustomed place beside the mizen rigging . . . his ringing cry ran through the vaulted hull, 'Stern all! the White Whale spouts thick blood!'"

151 Chapter CXII: The Blacksmith. ". . . Perth, the begrimed, blistered old blacksmith . . . A peculiar walk in this old man, a certain slight but painful appearing yawing in his gait, had at an early period of the voyage excited the curiosity of the mariners . . . so it came to pass that every one now knew the shameful story of his wretched fate. Belated, and not innocently, one bitter winter's midnight, on the road running between two country towns, the blacksmith half-stupidly felt the deadly numbness stealing over him, and sought refuge in a leaning, dilapidated barn. The issue was, the loss of the extremities of both feet . . . He had been an artisan of famed excellence . . . owned a house and garden; embraced a youthful, daughter-like, loving wife, and three blithe, ruddy children . . . But one night, under cover of darkness, and further concealed in a most-cunning disguisement, a desperate burglar slid into his happy home, and robbed them all of everything . . . It was the Bottle Conjurer! Upon the opening of that fatal cork, forth flew the fiend, and shriveled up his home . . . the house was sold; the mother dived down into the long, church-yard grass; her children twice followed her thither; and the houseless, familyless old man staggered off a vagabond . . . from the hearts of infinite Pacifics, the thousand mermaids sing to him . . . so Perth went a-whaling."

152 Chapter CXIII: The Forge. ". . . Ahab, passionately advancing, and leaning with both hands on Perth's shoulders; 'look ye here—*here*—can ye smoothe out a seam like this, blacksmith,' sweeping one had across his ribbed brow . . . 'I, too, want a harpoon made; one that a thousand yoke of fiends could not part, Perth . . . Look ye, blacksmith, these

are the gathered nail-stubs of the steel shoes of racing horses . . . But now for the barbs; thou must make them thyself, man. Here are my razors—the best of steel; here, and make the barbs sharp as the needle-sleet of the Icy Sea . . . Take them, man, I have no need for them; for I now neither shave, sup, nor pray till—but here—to work! No, no—no water for that; I want it of the true death-temper. Ahoy, there! Tashtego, Queequeg, Daggoo! What say ye, pagans! Will ye give me as much blood as will cover this barb?' holding it high up. A cluster of dark nods replied, Yes. Three punctures were made in the heathen flesh, and the White Whale's barbs were then tempered."

153 Chapter CXIV: The Gilder. "Penetrating further and further into the heart of the Japanese cruising ground, the Pequod was soon all astir in the fishery . . . At such times, under an abated sun; afloat all day upon smooth, slow heaving swells . . . these are the times of dreamy quietude, when beholding the tranquil beauty and brilliancy of the ocean's skin, one forgets the tiger heart that pants beneath it; and would not willingly remember, that this velvety paw conceals a remorseless fang . . . And Stubb, fish-like, with sparkling scales, leaped up in that same golden light;—'I am Stubb, and Stubb has his history; but here Stubb takes oaths that he has always been jolly!'"

154 Chapter CXV: The Pequod Meets the Bachelor. "It was a Nantucket ship, the Bachelor, which had just wedged in her last cask of oil, and bolted down her bursting hatches . . . Sideways lashed in each of her three basketed tops were two barrels of sperm; above which, in her top-mast cross-trees, you saw slender breakers of the same precious fluid; and nailed to her main truck was a brazen lamp. As was afterwards learned, the Bachelor had met with the most suprising success . . . additional supplemental casks had been bartered for from the ships she had met; and these

were stowed along the deck, and in the captain's and offi-cer's state-rooms . . . 'Come aboard, come aboard!' cried the gay Bachelor's commander, lifting a glass and a bottle in the air . . . 'Hast seen the White Whale?' gritted Ahab in reply . . . 'Thou art too damned jolly. Sail on. Hast lost any men?' . . . And thus, while the one ship went cheerily before the breeze, the other stubbornly fought against it; and so the two vessels parted."

155 Chapter CXVI: The Dying Whale. "For next day after encountering the gay Bachelor, whales were seen and four were slain; and one of them by Ahab . . . Soothed again, but only soothed to deeper gloom, Ahab, who had sterned off from the whale, sat intently watching his final wanings from the now tranquil boat. For that strange spec-tacle observable in all Sperm Whales dying—the turning sunwards of the head, and so expiring . . . 'He too worships fire; most faithful, broad, baronial vassal of the sun!—Oh that these too-favoring eyes should see these too-favoring sights. Look! here, far water-locked . . . here, too, life dies sunwards full of faith; but see! no sooner dead, than death whirls round the corpse, and it heads some other way' . . ."

156 Chapter CXVII: The Whale Watch. ". . . the windward [whale] could not be reached till morning; and the boat that had killed it lay by its side all night; and that boat was Ahab's . . . Started from his slumbers, Ahab, face to face, saw the Parsee . . . 'I have dreamed it again," said [Ahab] . . . 'Of the hearses? Have I not said, old man, that neither hearse nor coffin can be thine? . . . ere thou couldst die on this voyage, two hearses must verily be seen by thee on the sea; the first not made by mortal hands; and the visible wood of the last one must be grown in America . . . Hemp only can kill thee.' . . . 'The gallows, ye mean.—I am immortal then, on land and on sea,' cried Ahab, with a laugh of derision . . ."

Appendix

157 Chapter CXVII: The Quadrant. "The season for the Line at length grew near . . . eager mariners . . . impatient for the order to point the ship's prow for the Equator . . . It was hard upon high noon; and Ahab, seated in the bows of his high-hoisted boat, was about taking his wonted daily observation of the sun to determine his latitude . . . he again looked up towards the sun and murmured to himself: 'Thou sea-mark! thou high and mightly Pilot! thou tellest me truly where I *am*—but canst thou cast the least hint where I *shall* be? Or canst thou tell where some other thing besides me is this moment living? Where is Moby Dick? . . . Then gazing at his quadrant . . . 'Foolish toy! babies' plaything of haughty admirals, and commodores, and captains; the word brags of thee, of thy cunning and might; but what after all canst thou do . . . Thou canst not tell where one drop of water or one grain of sand will be to-morrow noon; and yet with thy impotence thou insulteth the sun! Science! Curse thee, thou vain toy! . . . Curse thee, thou quadrant!' dashing it to the deck . . . and thus trampled with his live and dead feet . . . till Ahab, troubledly pacing the deck, shouted out—'To the braces! Up helm!—square in!'"

158 Chapter CXIX: The Candles. ". . . in these resplendent Japanese seas the mariner encounters the direst of all storms, the Typhoon . . . When darkness came on, sky and sea roared and split with the thunder, and blazed with the lightning . . . A great rolling sea, dashing high up against the reeling ship's high tetering side, stove in the boat's bottom at the stern, and left it again, all dripping through like a sieve . . . 'Look aloft!' cried Starbuck. 'The St. Elmo's Lights (corpus sancti) corposants! the corposants!' All the yardarms were tipped with a pallid fire; and touched at each tripointed lightning-rod-end with three tapering white flames, each of the three tall masts was silently burning in that sulphurous air, like three gigantic wax tapers before an altar . . . Ahab's harpoon, the one forged at Perth's fire, remained

firmly lashed in its conspicuous crotch . . . but the sea that had stove its bottom had caused the loose leather sheath to drop off; and from the keen steel barb there now came a levelled flame of pale, forked fire. As the silent harpoon burned there like a serpent's tongue . . . dashing the rattling lightning links to the deck, and snatching the burning harpoon, Ahab waved it like a torch . . . And with one blast of his breath he extinguished the flame."

159 Chapter CXX: The Deck Towards the End of the First Night Watch. "[*Ahab standing by the helm. Starbuck approaching him.*] 'We must send down the main-top-sail yard, Sir. The band is working loose, and the lee lift is half-stranded. Shall I strike it, Sir?' 'Strike nothing; lash it . . . Strike nothing, and stir nothing, but lash everything . . . Oh, none but cowards send down their brain-trucks in tempest time. What a hooroosh aloft there! I would e'en take it for sublime, did I not know that the colic is a noisy malady. Oh, take medicine, take medicine!'"

160 Chapter CXXI: Midnight.—The Forecastle Bulwarks. ". . . 'Stubb . . . Didn't you once say that whatever ship Ahab sails in, that ship should pay something extra on its insurance policy' . . . 'Seems to me we are lashing down these anchors now as if they were never going to be used again. Tying these two anchors here, Flask, seems like tying a man's hands behind him . . . This is a nasty night, lad.'"

161 Chapter CXXII: Midnight Aloft.—Thunder and Lightning. "[*The main-top-sail yard.—Tashtego passing new lashings around it.*] 'Um, um, um. Stop that thunder! Plenty too much thunder up here. What's the use of thunder? Um, um, um. We don't want thunder; we want rum; give us a glass of rum. Um, um, um!'"

162 Chapter CXXIII: The Musket. ". . . Starbuck . . . mechanically went below to apprise Captain Ahab of the circum-

Appendix

stance . . . The loaded muskets in the rack were shiningly revealed . . . at the instant when he saw the muskets, there strangely evolved an evil thought . . . 'Does he not say he will not strike his spars upon any gale? Had he not dashed his heavenly quadrant? and in these same perilous seas, gropes he not his way by mere dead reckoning on the error-abounding log? and in this very Typhoon, did he not swear that he would have no lightning rods? . . . Yes, it would make him the willful murderer of thirty men and more . . . Ha! is he muttering in his sleep? Yes, just there,— in there, he's sleeping' . . . but turning from the door, he placed the death-tube in its rack, and left the place."

163 Chapter CXXIV: The Needle. "But suddenly reined back by some counter thought, he hurried towards the helm, huskily demanding how the ship was heading. 'East-sou-east, Sir,' said the frightened steersman. 'Thou liest!' smiting him with his clenched fist. 'Heading East at this hour in the morning, and the sun astern?' . . . lo! the two compasses pointed East, and the Pequod was infallibly going West . . . 'last night's thunder turned our compasses—that's all' . . . shouted out his orders for the ship's course to be changed accordingly. The yards were hard up; and once more the Pequod thrust her undaunted bows into the opposing wind . . . 'my men, the thunder turned old Ahab's needles; but out of this bit of steel Ahab can make one of his own, that will point as true as any.'"

164 Chapter CXXV: The Log and Line. "'Forward, there! Heave the log!' . . . the old Manxman, who was intently eyeing both him and the line, made bold to speak. 'Sir, I mistrust it; this line looks far gone, long heat and wet have spoiled it.' 'Up with it! So.' The log was heaved. The loose coils rapidly straightened out in a long dragging line astern . . . Snap! the overstrained line sagged down in one long festoon; the tugging log was gone."

165 Chapter CXXV: The Log and Line. "'Ha, Pip? come to help; eh, Pip?' 'Pip? whom call ye Pip? Pip jumped overboard from the whale-boat. Pip's missing . . . Ho! there's his arm just breaking water . . . here's Pip, trying to get on board again.' 'Peace, thou crazy loon,' cried the Manxman, seizing him by the arm. 'Away from the quarter-deck!' 'Here, boy; Ahab's cabin shall be Pip's home henceforth, while Ahab lives. Thou touchest my inmost centre, boy; thou art tied to me by cords woven of my heart-strings. Come, let's down.'"

166 Chapter CXXVI: The Life-Buoy. "At sun-rise this man went from his hammock to his mast-head at the fore; and whether it was that he was not yet half waked from his sleep . . . there is now no telling . . . he had not been long at his perch, when a cry was heard—a cry and a rushing—and looking up, they saw a falling phantom in the air; and looking down, a little tossed heap of white bubbles in the blue of the sea. The life-buoy—a long slender cask—was dropped from the stern, where it always hung obedient to a cunning spring; but no hand rose to seize it, and the sun having long beat upon this cask it had shrunken, so that it slowly filled . . . and the studded iron-bound cask followed the sailor to the bottom . . . The lost life-buoy was now to be replaced . . . Queequeg hinted a hint concerning his coffin . . . 'A life-buoy of a coffin!' cried Starbuck, starting . . . 'It will make a good enough one,' said Flask, 'the carpenter here can arrange it easily.'"

167 Chapter CXXVII: The Deck. "'Then tell me; art thou not an arrant, all-grasping, intermeddling, monopolizing, heathenish old scamp, to be one day making legs, and the next day coffins to clap them in, and yet again life-buoys out of those same coffins? Thou art as unprincipled as the gods, and as much of a jack-of-al-trades . . . A life-buoy of a coffin! Does it go further? Can it be that in some spiritual

sense the coffin is, after all, but an immortality-preserver! . . . Will ye never have done, Carpenter, with that accursed sound?'"

168 Chapter CXXVIII: The Pequod Meets the Rachel. "Next day, a large ship, the Rachel, was descried, bearing directly down upon the Pequod . . . 'Hast seen the White Whale?' 'Aye, yesterday. Have ye seen a whale-boat adrift?' . . . After a keen sail before the wind, this fourth boat—the swiftest keeled of all—seemed to have succeeded in fastening . . . In the distance [Captain Gardiner] saw the diminished dotted boat . . . it was concluded that the stricken whale must have indefinitely run away with his pursuers, as often happens . . . 'My boy, my own boy is among them. For God's sake—I beg, I conjure . . . let me charter your ship' . . . the stranger was still beseeching his poor boon of Ahab; and Ahab still stood like an anvil, receiving every shock without the least quivering of his own . . . 'Captain Gardiner, I will not do it. Even now I lose time. Good bye, good bye . . . may I forgive myself, but I must go.' Soon the two ships diverged wakes . . ."

169 Chapter CXXIX: The Cabin. "[*Ahab moving to go on deck; Pip catches him by the hand to follow.*] 'Lad, lad, I tell thee thou must not follow Ahab now . . . Like cures like; and for this hunt, my malady becomes my most desired health.' . . . 'No, no, no! ye have not a whole body, Sir; do ye but use poor me for your one lost leg; only tread upon me, Sir; I ask no more, so I remain a part of ye.' 'Oh! spite of million villains, this makes me a bigot in the fadeless fidelity of man!—and a black! and crazy!—but methinks like-cures-like applies to him too; he grows so sane again . . . Weep so, and I will murder thee! have a care, for Ahab too is mad.'"

170 Chapter CXXX: The Hat. "But when three or four days had slided by, after meeting the children-seeking Rachel; and

no spout had yet been seen; the monomaniac old man seemed distrustful of his crew's fidelity . . . 'I will have the first sight of the whale myself.'—he said. 'Aye! Ahab must have the doubloon!' . . . he gave the word for them to hoist him to his perch . . . And thus, with one hand clinging round the royal mast, Ahab gazed abroad upon the sea for miles and miles . . . ere he had been there ten minutes; one of those red-billed savage sea-hawks which so often fly incommodiously close round the manned mast-heads of whalemen in these latitudes; one of those birds came wheeling and screaming round his head . . . 'Your hat, your hat, Sir!' . . . with a scream, the black hawk darted away with his prize."

171 Chapter CXXXI: The Pequod Meets the Delight. "Upon the stranger's shears were beheld the shattered, white ribs, and some few splintered planks, of what had once been a whale-boat . . . sadly glancing upon a rounded hammock on the deck, whose gathered sides some noiseless sailors were busy in sewing together . . . 'I bury but one of five stout men, who were alive only yesterday; but were dead ere night. Only that one I bury; the rest were buried before they died; you sail upon their tomb.' . . . But the suddenly started Pequod was not quick enough to escape the sound of the splash that the corpse soon made as it struck the sea; not so quick, indeed, but that some of the flying bubbles might have sprinkled her hull with their ghostly baptism."

172 Chapter CXXXII: The Symphony. 'I struck my first whale—a boy-harpooner of eighteen! Forty—forty—forty years ago—ago! Forty years of continual whaling! . . . forty years on the pitiless sea! for forty years has Ahab forsaken the peaceful land, for forty years to make war on the horrors of the deep! Aye and yes, Starbuck, out of those forty years I have not spent three ashore . . . from that young girl-wife

I wedded past fifty, and sailed for Cape Horn the next day, leaving but one dent in my marriage pillow—wife? wife?—rather a widow with her husband alive! . . . the boy vivaciously wakes; sits up in bed; and his mother tells him of me; of cannibal old me; how I am abroad upon the deep . . . What is it, what nameless, inscrutable, unearthly thing is it; what cozening, hidden lord and master, and cruel, remorseless emperor commands me; that against all natural lovings and longings, I so keep pushing, and crowding, and jamming myself on all the time . . . '"

173 Chapter CXXXIII: The Chase—First Day. ". . . a gull-like cry in the air, 'There she blows!—there she blows! A hump like a snow-hill! It is Moby Dick!' . . . Soon all boats but Starbuck's were dropped . . . the tall but shattered pole of a recent lance projected from the White Whale's back; and at intervals one of the cloud of soft-toed fowls hovering, and to and fro skimming like a canopy over the fish, silently perched and rocked on this pole . . . But soon the fore part of him slowly rose from the water; for an instant his whole marbleized body formed a high arch, like Virginia's Natural Bridge, and warningly waving his banered flukes in the air, the grand god revealed himself, sounded, and went out of sight . . ."

174 Chapter CXXXIII: The Chase—First Day. "But suddenly as [Ahab] peered down and down into its depths, he profoundly saw a white living spot no bigger than a white weasel, with wonderful celerity uprising, and magnifying as it rose, till it turned, and then there were plainly revealed two long crooked rows of white, glistening teeth, floating up from the undiscoverable bottom. It was Moby Dick's open mouth and scrolled jaw; his vast, shadowed bulk still half blending with the blue of the sea. The glittering mouth yawned beneath the boat like an open-doored marble tomb . . . in the manner of a biting shark, slowly and

feelingly taking its bows full within his mouth, so that the long, narrow, scrolled lower jaw curled high up into the open air, and one of the teeth caught in a row-lock . . . the frail gun-wales bent in, collapsed, and snapped, as both jaws, like an enormous shears, sliding further aft, bit the craft completely in twain . . . But only slipping further into the whale's mouth, and tilting over sideways as it slipped, the boat had shaked off his hold on the jaw; spilled [Ahab] out of it, as he leaned to the push; and so he fell flat-faced upon the sea . . . But soon resuming his horizontal attitude, Moby Dick swam swiftly round and round the wrecked crew; sideways churning the water in his vengeful wake, as if lashing himself up to still another and more deadly assault . . . The Peqoud's prows were pointed; and breaking up the charmed circle, she effectually parted the White Whale from his victim. As he sullenly swam off, the boats flew to the rescue . . . like the double-jointed wings of an albatross, the Pequod bore down in the leeward wake of Moby Dick."

175 Chapter CXXXIV: The Chase—Second Day. "The ship tore on; leaving such a furrow in the sea as when a cannon-ball, misspent, becomes a plough-share and turns up the level field . . . The frenzies of the chase had by this time worked them bubbingly up, like old wine worked anew . . . That hand of Fate had snatched their souls; and by the stirring perils of the previous day; the rack of the past night's suspense; the fixed, unfearing, blind, reckless way in which their wild craft went plunging towards its flying mark . . . They were one man, not thirty . . . The rigging lived. The mast-heads, like the tops of tall palms, were outspreadingly tufted with arms and legs. Clinging to a spar with one hand, some reached forth the other with impatient wavings; others, shading their eyes from the vivid sunlight, sat far out on the rocking yards; all the spars in full bearing of mortals, ready and ripe for their fate."

Appendix

176 Chapter CXXXIV: The Chase—Second Day. ". . . much nearer to the ship than the place of the imaginary jet, less than a mile ahead—Moby Dick bodily burst into view! For not by any calm and indolent spoutings . . . but by the far more wondrous phenomenon of breaching. Rising with his utmost velocity from the furthest depths, the Sperm Whale thus booms his entire bulk into the pure element of air, and piling up a mountain of dazzling foam, shows his place to the distance of seven miles and more . . . the White Whale tossed himself salmon-like to heaven . . . intolerably glittered and glared like a glacier . . . 'Aye, breach your last to the sun, Moby Dick!' cried Ahab, 'thy hour and thy harpoon are at hand!' . . ."

177 Chapter CXXXIV: The Chase—Second Day. "As if to strike a quick terror into them . . . Moby Dick had turned, and was now coming for the three crews . . . heedless of the irons darted at him from every boat, seemed only intent on annihilating each separate plank . . . in his untraceable evolutions, the White Whale so crossed and recrossed, and in a thousand ways entangled the slack of the three lines now fast to him . . . the White Whale made a sudden rush among the remaining tangles of the others lines; by so doing, irresistibly dragged the more involved boats of Stubb and Flask towards his flukes; dashed them together like two rolling husks on a surf-beaten beach . . . Ahab's yet unstricken boat seemed drawn up towards heaven by the sea, the White Whale dashed his broad forehead against its bottom, and sent it, turning over and over, into the air; till it fell again—gunwale downwards . . . Upon mustering the company, the Parsee was not there . . . 'caught among the tangles of [Ahab's] line—I thought I saw him dragging under.'"

178 Chapter CXXXV: The Chase—Third Day. "'Nothing! and noon at hand! . . . Aye, aye, it must be so. I've oversailed

him. How got the start? Aye, he's chasing me now; not I, him—that's bad; I might have known it, too. Fool! The lines—the harpoons he's towing.'"

179 Chapter CXXXV: The Chase—Third Day. ". . . now being pointed in the reverse direction, the braced ship sailed hard upon the breeze as she rechurned the cream in her own white wake . . . In due time the boats were lowered . . . 'Starbuck. I am old;—shake hands with me, man.' Their hands met; their eyes fastened; Starbuck's tears the glue."

180 Chapter CXXXV: The Chase—Third Day. ". . . numbers of sharks, seemingly rising from out the dark waters beneath the hull, maliciously snapped at the blades of the oars . . . A low rumbling sound was heard; a subterraneous hum; and then all held their breaths; as bedraggled with trailing ropes, and harpoons, and lances, a vast form shot length-wise, but obliquely from the sea . . . Lashed round and round to the fish's back; pinioned in the turns upon turns in which, during the past night, the whale had reeled the involutions of the lines around him, the half torn body of the Parsee was seen; his sable raiment frayed to shreds; his distended eyes turned full upon old Ahab . . . 'this then is the hearse that thou didst promise.' . . ."

181 Chapter CXXXV: The Chase—Third Day. ". . . as head on, [Moby Dick] came churning his tail among the boats; and once more flailed them apart; spilling out irons and lances from the two mates' boats, and dashing in one side or the upper part of the bows, but leaving Ahab's almost without a scar . . . Moby Dick was now again steadily swimming forward; and had almost passed the ship . . . He seemed swimming with his utmost velocity, and now only intent upon pursuing his own straight path in the sea. 'Oh, Ahab,' cried Starbuck, 'not too late is it, even now, the third day, to desist. See! Moby Dick seeks thee not. It is thou, thou, that madly seeketh him!'"

Appendix

182 Citation lost.

183 Chapter CXXXV: The Chase—Third Day. ". . . Stubb and Flask, busying themselves on deck among bundles of new irons and lances . . . now marking that the vane or flag was gone from the main-mast-head, [Ahab] shouted to Tashtego, who had just gained that perch, to descend again for another flag, and a hammer and nails, and so nail it to the mast . . . the unpitying sharks accompanied him; and so pertinaciously stuck to the boat; and so continually bit at the plying oars, that the blades became jagged and crunched, and left small splinters in the sea, at almost every dip . . ."

184 Chapter CXXXV: The Chase—Third Day. ". . . Ahab was fairly within the smoky mountain mist, which, thrown off from the whale's spout, curled round his great, Monadnock hump; he was even thus close to him; when, with body arched back, and both arms lengthwise high-lifted to the poise, he darted his fierce iron, and his far fiercer curse into the hated whale. As both steel and curse sank to the socket, as if sucked into a morass, Moby Dick sideways writhed; spasmodically rolled his nigh flank against the bow, and, without staving a hole in it, so suddenly canted the boat over, that had it not been for the elevated part of the gunwale to which he clung, Ahab would once more have been tossed into the sea . . . the third man helplessly dropping astern, but still afloat and swimming . . . the White Whale darted through the weltering sea. But when Ahab cried out to the steersman to take new turns with the line, and hold it so; and commanded the crew to turn round on their seats, and tow the boat up to the mark; the moment the treacherous line felt that doubt strain and tug, it snapped in the empty air!"

185 Chapter CXXXV: The Chase—Third Day. "Hearing the tremendous rush of the sea-crashing boat, the whale wheeled round to present his blank forehead at bay; but in that evolution, catching sight of the nearing black hull of the ship; seemingly seeing in it the source of all his persecutions; bethinking it—it may be—a larger and nobler foe; of a sudden, he bore down upon its advancing prow, smiting his jaws amid fiery showers of foam . . . the sold white buttress of his forehead smote the ship's starboard bow, till men and timbers reeled. Some fell flat upon their faces. Like dislodged trucks, the heads of the harpooners aloft shook on their bull-like necks. Through the breach, they heard the waters pour, as mountain torrents down a flume. 'The ship! The hearse!—the second hearse!' cried Ahab from the boat . . ."

186 Chapter CXXXV: The Chase—Third Day. "Diving beneath the settling ship, the whale ran quivering along its keel; but turning under water, swiftly shot to the surface again, far off the other bow, but within a few yards of Ahab's boat, where, for a time, he lay quiescent . . . 'Towards thee I roll, thou all destroying but unconquering whale; to the last I grapple with thee; from hell's heart I stab at thee; for hate's sake I spit my last breath at thee. Sink all coffins and all hearses to one common pool! and since neither can be mine, let me tow to pieces, while still chasing thee, though tied to thee, thou damned whale! *Thus*, I give up the spear!' The harpoon was darted; the stricken whale flew forward; with igniting velocity the line ran through the groove;—ran foul. Ahab stooped to clear it; he did clear it; but the flying turn caught him round the neck, and voicelessly as Turkish mutes bowstring their victim, he was shot out of the boat, ere the crew knew he was gone. Next instant, the heavy eye-splice in the rope's final end flew out of the stark-empty tub, knocked down an oarsman, and smiting the sea, disappeared in its depths."

187 Chapter CXXXV: The Chase—Third Day. "For an instant, the tranced boat's crew stood still; then turned, 'The ship? Great God, where is the ship?' Soon they through dim, bewildering mediums saw her sidelong fading phantom, as in the gaseous Fata Morgana; only the uppermost masts out of water . . . And now, concentric circles seized the lone boat itself, and all its crew, and each floating oar, and every lance-pole, and spinning, animate and inanimate, all round and round in one vortex, carried the smallest chip of the Pequod out of sight."

188 Chapter CXXXV: The Chase—Third Day. "But as the last whelmings intermixingly poured themselves over the sunken head of the Indian at the main-mast, leaving a few inches of the erect spar yet visible . . . A sky hawk that tauntingly had followed the main-truck downwards from its natural home among the stars, pecking at the flag, and incommoding Tashtego there; this bird now chanced to intercept its broad fluttering wing between the hammer and the wood; and simultaneously feeling that etherial thrill, the submerged savage beneath, in his death-grasp, kept his hammer frozen there; and so the bird of heaven, with archangelic shrieks, and his imperial beak thrust upwards, and his whole captive form folded in the flag of Ahab, went down with his ship . . . and the great shroud of the sea rolled on as it rolled five thousand years ago."

189 Epilogue. ". . . one did survive the wreck . . . I was he whom the Fates ordained to take the place of Ahab's bowsman . . . was dropped astern . . . rising with great force, the coffin life-buoy shot lengthwise from the sea, fell over, and floated by my side. Buoyed up by that coffin, for almost one whole day and night, I floated on a soft and dirge-like main."

190 Epilogue. "On the second day, a sail drew near, nearer, and picked me up at last. It was the devious-cruising Rachel,

that in her retracing search after her missing children, only found another orphan."